HOLY CHOW

ALSO BY DAVID ROSENFELT

HOLY CHOW

David Rosenfelt

MINOTAUR BOOKS

NEW YORK

First published in the United States by Minotaur Books,
an imprint of St. Martin's Publishing Group

HOLY CHOW. Copyright © 2022 by Tara Productions, Inc.
All rights reserved. Printed in the United States of America.
For information, address St. Martin's Publishing Group,
120 Broadway, New York, NY 10271.

www.minotaurbooks.com

Library of Congress Cataloging-in-Publication Data

Names: Rosenfelt, David, author.
Title: Holy chow / David Rosenfelt.
Description: First Edition. | New York : Minotaur Books, 2022. |
    Series: An Andy Carpenter Novel ; 25
Identifiers: LCCN 2022010217 | ISBN 9781250828873 (hardcover) |
    ISBN 9781250828880 (ebook)
Classification: LCC PS3618.O838 H65 2022 | DDC 813/.6—dc23
LC record available at https://lccn.loc.gov/2022010217

Our books may be purchased in bulk for promotional, educational,
or business use. Please contact your local bookseller or the Macmillan
Corporate and Premium Sales Department at 1-800-221-7945, extension
5442, or by email at MacmillanSpecialMarkets@macmillan.com.

First Edition: 2022

10 9 8 7 6 5 4 3 2 1

HOLY CHOW

Matt Reisinger knew what he needed and when he needed it.

It was the key to his business success. Most executives on his level would credit some business mentor, or perhaps a parent, or maybe a business school professor, as the person who most helped them along the way.

Not Matt. Without question, in his mind the individual most responsible for his professional achievements was Mother Nature.

Twice a year Matt would drive from his Cincinnati home to the mountains of North Carolina. He always chose to drive, though as the CEO of a company that supplied private planes to wealthy clients, he obviously could easily and comfortably have traveled by air.

Driving was part of the mental cleansing; it was the time in which he made the transfer from his high-pressure job to his period of freedom. By the time he arrived at the mountains, his head was clear and he had put the real world behind him.

These trips had an irony that always became clear to him afterward, yet always surprised him. Even though he almost never thought about business or his job while he was there, he always returned with a bunch of ideas and new strategies.

Obviously, clearing his mind left space to think in fresh ways.

He even thought about mandating these kinds of outings for the executives under him, but decided that it was impractical, and also that not everyone was likely to react in the same way.

He always stayed up on the mountains for four days, hiking and camping. He brought all the supplies he would need with him in the car, since it was not the kind of place where you can run in to a Walmart. He never varied this routine, which had served him well over the years.

Matt's life was privileged; it had always been. He was born into a reasonably wealthy family, had been taught the value of money and ambition, and had done what he needed to maintain his lifestyle. But up on the mountain, none of that mattered; he was like everyone else, dealing with the elements and the difficulties that the wilderness presented, and that appealed to him on a basic level.

He was in the third day on this current trip, which was typically the day when he started dreading his return to the real world. That dread usually peaked on the fourth day and then started to wane, and by the time he'd driven back home he would always be refreshed and enthusiastic.

But this trip and this time were different. He was dealing with business and personal challenges he had never before faced, yet he had resolved to confront them. It might change his life, but he could not turn away from these challenges.

Matt always slept on the inside of the trail, away from the ledge. He didn't have a fear of heights, but he did have a healthy respect for them. He was not prone to walking in his sleep, but there was no sense taking any chances.

Matt woke up and, as he had on the previous two days, made a fire, cooked himself breakfast and made coffee. Every day in North Carolina breakfast was the same . . . bacon, eggs, and oatmeal . . . and plenty of coffee. That was true of Matt both on the mountain and in the office: he required copious amounts of coffee.

"Is that real coffee? Or am I dreaming?"

Matt looked up to see another hiker. This big guy was obviously in good shape, and he carried a large backpack with ease. He had a smile on his face and made eye contact with Matt, though the stranger occasionally glanced eagerly at the coffeepot.

"It's real," Matt said. "I'm guessing you'd like some?"

"I'll trade you two protein bars and an apple. If necessary I'll throw in my firstborn. I forgot to bring coffee with me, the first and last time that will ever happen."

"Well, I can't make you a nonfat, no-foam venti latte, but I can definitely give you some black coffee. No trade necessary."

Matt didn't tell him his name or shake his hand. Those were unnecessary courtesies up here; they knew they would never see each other again. But Matt was happy to supply coffee and make this guy's time on the mountain easier and more pleasant; that was the way that things were done in this world.

The way they should be done in every world.

He poured the guy a cup of coffee and handed it to him. The stranger reached for it with his left hand and punched Matt in the face with his right. The punch traveled less than a foot, but was tremendously powerful.

Matt quite literally never saw it coming and was never able to reflect on it because he instantly lost consciousness. His face was badly bruised and starting to bleed, but the stranger was not concerned about that because plenty of bruising and bleeding was to follow.

No one would ever be able to determine that this blow was the first damage to Matt's body. No coroner in the world was that good.

The stranger looked around to make sure that no other hikers were within sight, though he had already scouted out the area. He quickly put on gloves, so as not to leave fingerprints, then gathered all of Matt's stuff and repacked it, leaving it not far from the ledge.

He almost effortlessly picked up Matt's unconscious body and tossed it over the ledge. There was no way to tell when Matt actually died from the impacts he made along the way, but that wouldn't matter to anyone, least of all the stranger.

There would be no reason to suspect foul play, and certainly no way to prove it. Matt was a hiker who for a horrible moment was not careful, and who had paid for it with his life.

In everyone's eyes, it would just look as if Matt had lost a battle with Mother Nature.

Mr. Carpenter, this is Rachel Morehouse. I don't know if you remember me."

My memory seems to fail me every day; for example, I should start walking my cell phone on a leash to remember where I've put it. But I definitely remember Rachel Morehouse.

"Of course I do. How are you, Rachel?"

"I'm fine, thank you."

"Is there a problem with Lion?" I clutch the phone a bit tighter. I do not want there to be a problem with Lion. He is a magnificent dog, a chow chow, and we named him Lion because his looks reminded me of the Cowardly Lion in *The Wizard of Oz*.

Lion is the reason I am able to find Rachel in my depleted memory bank. One day about a year ago she walked into the Tara Foundation, the dog rescue group that I run with my partner, Willie Miller. She saw Lion and fell in love, adopting him immediately.

Until that day Lion had been a bit of a problem for us. Not only was he large and approaching senior age, two qualities that made placing him in a home more difficult, but he had an alleged biting incident in his past. That made it much more difficult, and we had him for almost six weeks. I was afraid his wait to find a loving home would drag on forever.

But enter Rachel Morehouse, a tiny woman in her sixties who looked comical next to Lion. He was almost as big as she was, and when they left, it was hard to tell who was walking whom.

She said that she had lost her husband a while back and was all alone. She wanted a dog who needed her and who she could love and care for the rest of his life. Lion fit the bill perfectly; and right now I'm afraid that something might have happened to change that.

"Oh, no, Lion is fine," she says. "Wonderful, actually. More than wonderful."

"I'm glad to hear that; you had me worried for a minute."

"Sorry, but Lion is the reason I am calling."

"You want a brother for him? Or maybe a sister? That would not be a problem."

She laughs. "No, but I do want to make sure he's taken care of."

"You're losing me." People seem to lose me a lot these days; my wife, Laurie, thinks I should wear a collar with a name tag or maybe tie a bell around my neck.

"People don't live forever, Andy. If something happened to me, I want to make sure Lion is cared for."

"Oh. So you'd want me to take him? And find him a great home? That I can guarantee." I'm not sure what I was expecting her to say, but this is an easy promise.

"Thank you; I knew you would. But you're in second position; my stepson is coming to visit; I'm going to ask him as well."

"Whatever you need, Rachel. Does your stepson like dogs? Because Lion is a lot of dog."

She laughs again; Rachel Morehouse has a great laugh. "You know something? I don't know. I'm trying to reestablish our relationship. Family, Andy. You know how that can be."

Actually, I don't, at least not firsthand. My family relationships have always been comparatively good, but obviously there have been issues in Rachel's. I don't know what they are, and I'm not about to ask.

"Well, I'm here if you need me. But I sure as hell hope it's a long time before you do."

"So do I, Andy." Her tone is suddenly serious. "So do I."

Opening day has always excited me.

Going with my father to the season opener at Yankee Stadium, as we did every year, was a tradition that in my mind stood out above all others. Even when I became a Yankee hater, in the George Steinbrenner / Billy Martin era, I just switched over to the Mets and went to their first game every year instead.

Today's opening day is a bit different, but every bit as exciting, maybe even more so. My son, Ricky, is a pitcher and shortstop on his Little League team, and today they are starting the season by playing Clifton at Eastside Park.

My wife, Laurie, and I are here to watch Ricky in action, and she is almost as proud and excited as I am. He'll be going to overnight camp soon, so won't get to play in many of these games, which only heightens the anticipation today. Only one thing is putting a damper on the day, and that is the coach, Frank Vandeweghe.

His philosophy is that all the kids should play, that they are here to have fun and that winning is not the main objective. He believes that eleven- and twelve-year-olds need to learn sportsmanship; he doesn't want to step on Clifton's tiny necks and crush their souls.

The man is clearly an idiot.

That idiocy has never been more evident than today. Ricky is starting the game on the bench. A Carpenter on the bench! The coach has told him that this other kid is going to pitch the first three innings, and that Ricky will pitch the next three.

"What's the difference?" Laurie asks me when I express my outrage to her.

"What's the difference? What if there are major-league scouts here? How will it look if he can't even start in Little League?"

"You think there are major-league scouts here to watch this game?"

"You never know. They start really young."

"I think the coach has the right attitude," Laurie says. "There's too much emphasis placed on winning."

"What are you talking about? Winning is why they keep score. Without winners nobody would know who the losers are. Fans would never boo; coaches would never get fired. It would be chaos. Winning makes the world go round."

Keeping score today turns out not to be such a good idea, as those Clifton animals beat Paterson by a score of 14–6. Ricky gives up eight of the runs.

When the game ends, Laurie says, "It's just as well that there were no major-league scouts here."

"Ricky's not a relief pitcher," I say. "He's a starter. Not starting threw him off. And those Clifton kids were ringers; half of them were over age."

"Andy . . ."

"I'm telling you, that catcher had to be at least thirty. He probably shaved twenty minutes before the game. His wife and kids were in the stands."

Ricky and his friend Will Rubenstein, who is the team's starting third baseman, come over after the coach gives them their postgame pep talk. Will's father, Brian, is a pediatrician and couldn't leave his office to see the game.

"Good game, guys," Laurie says, completely misrepresenting what happened.

"We lost, Mom," Ricky says.

"But you played hard. You want to go for pizza?"

The prospect of pizza appeals to them, so we head to Patsy's, easily the best pizza place around. If the kids are upset by the result of the game, they're hiding it well, so I feign a good mood as well. By the time we're finished laughing through dinner, I don't even have to feign it.

We drop Will off at his house and head home. We live on Forty-second Street in Paterson, not far from the park. Once Will is out of the car, I say to Ricky, "You looked good out there on the mound."

"Good? I gave up seven runs." But he doesn't seem that concerned; maybe he knows the major-league scouts didn't show up.

"Eight," I say, as Laurie shoots me a dirty look. So I try to fix it. "But one of them was unearned."

When we get home, Ricky goes off to do his homework, and I take the dogs for a walk. We have three, starting with Tara, a golden retriever who is the greatest dog of all time. She is the Willie Mays of dogs. We also have Sebastian, a basset hound whose main hobbies are sleeping and eating. There are anvils more active than Sebastian. Finally there's Hunter, a pug who worships Tara and does everything she does.

The four of us go back to Eastside Park, the scene of Ricky's baseball humiliation, though we don't go to the lower level where the field is. Instead we stay up top, near the tennis courts. We have to walk slowly, much to Tara's dismay, because Sebastian regards walking as something to be done with extreme reluctance.

When we get back, Laurie is on the phone, and I hear her say, "He just walked in." She hands me the phone. "It's Bernie Hudson."

Bernie Hudson is an attorney with a firm in Manhattan. He does mostly estate stuff for high-end clients. He lives in Teaneck, and Laurie and I have been out to dinner with Bernie and his wife a few times. I would categorize him as a friend, but not a close one.

We make small talk for a couple of minutes. For me, a small-talk minute is equivalent to an hour; I hate it and am bad at it. Finally I cut it off by saying, "So what's going on, Bernie?"

"Our firm represented Rachel Morehouse."

I'm surprised to hear this; Bernie's firm would be unlikely to handle anyone without significant money, and I have no reason to believe Rachel is wealthy, though I never thought about it either way.

What I notice first, though, is his use of the past tense, "represented." "You don't represent her anymore?"

"Well, we handle the estate, and . . . You didn't know that she passed away last week?"

"Damn . . . no, I didn't. I just spoke with her a few weeks ago."

"Oh, sorry . . . I thought you would have read about it."

I guess Bernie thinks I read the obituaries. "No, I didn't. Is this about her dog?"

"Her dog?" This leads me to believe that he has no idea what I'm talking about. "I don't know anything about her dog."

"Then why are you calling?"

"The reading of the will is tomorrow at our office at ten A.M. I've been notifying the beneficiaries, and you are apparently one of them. Obviously you are not required to be there."

"She asked me to take her dog if she passed away and her stepson didn't want it. Can I just get the dog? She rescued him from our foundation."

"Andy, I've told you all I can; I'm also the executor, so as you know, I'm bound to secrecy until the will is read. If it's about a dog, that will be part of the will. I don't know whether the dog will be there tomorrow, but if he is, and if she left him to you, I suppose you can take him."

"Okay."

"So will you be there?"

"I guess so. Who else would bring the biscuits?"

Rachel Morehouse, adopter of Lion, was worth at least $12 billion.

Based on what Google tells me, that is a conservative estimate. Her late husband was Stanley Wasserman, who ran one of the nation's largest private equity companies.

A switch to Wikipedia tells me that Rachel did something unusual with her name. While many women might take their husband's name but also keep their own as a middle name, in this case Rachel did the opposite. She adopted the name Rachel Wasserman Morehouse, relegating *Wasserman* to the middle position.

That's one of the reasons I didn't realize who she was. The other is that she didn't act like a billionaire at all. She drove up in what I think was a Chevy SUV, and if she dressed expensively or wore fancy jewelry, I didn't notice it. Of course, she could probably have worn the Hope Diamond and I would have missed it. Still, I admit I'm pretty shocked to learn about her wealth now.

Rachel inherited her deceased husband's estate, which included a controlling interest in Wasserman Equities. Stanley Wasserman was said to be a business genius, but he was clearly not particularly creative at naming companies.

Based on the articles I find in a few financial magazines,

Rachel surprised the business world by taking an active role in running the companies. It had been thought that she'd be an absentee, silent owner or would sell the business, perhaps to the two top executives already there. That's not what happened.

News reports say she was found in her home by her stepson, Anthony Wasserman. No cause of death is listed, but there is no intimation that it was from anything other than natural causes.

Armed with this information, none of which has any real meaning to me, I head to Bernie's office in Manhattan for the reading of the will. It is sort of an old tradition; there is no reason for anyone to actually attend. It's not like a raffle where you stand up and triumphantly hold up the winning ticket. Any beneficiaries will get their proceeds whether they are there or not.

I'm only going because I want to take Lion back with me. I don't know where he is, but I want to make sure he's not boarded somewhere in a cage. The sooner we get him back, the faster we can get him placed in a new home. I want to do that for Rachel, and I sure as hell want to do it for Lion. Of course, this will all change if Rachel's stepson wants Lion and promises to take good care of him.

Bernie's firm has its offices in Lower Manhattan, so for a 10:00 A.M. meeting I probably should leave my house in Paterson about two days before. But instead I leave at seven thirty, and miracle of miracles, the traffic in the Lincoln Tunnel is bad, but not horrendous, and I arrive at nine fifteen.

I have no idea how Bernie willingly makes this trek back and forth every day. It's a fifteen-minute drive from my house to my office on Van Houten Street in downtown Paterson, and it exhausts me. That is number 471 on the list of reasons why I try to avoid taking on clients.

Bernie's firm's offices feel sterile and, well, boring. I'm a criminal attorney, and even though I try to avoid work, when I do take on a case, I grudgingly find it interesting; it engages me. If I did something boring like estate law, then . . . it doesn't matter, because I would never do estate law. These offices look like they house people who do estate law.

I'm directed to the conference room where the reading is supposed to take place. It's enormous and contains the largest table I have ever seen; I cannot imagine how many trees gave their lives to create this table. It must take a cast of thousands to polish it and what seems like the four hundred chairs that surround it.

"Andy, come on in," Bernie says, even though I'm already in. We shake hands, and he introduces me to the only other person in the room. "Andy, meet Anthony Wasserman."

Wasserman, who is probably forty years old, stands, smiles, and offers his hand. "Tony," he says, correcting Bernie. "Tony Wasserman."

"Nice to meet you. I'm guessing that the fact that your name is Wasserman isn't a coincidence?"

Another smile. "No, Stanley was my father. Rachel was my stepmother."

"Sorry for your loss. She seemed like a great lady."

People are starting to file into the room, but no one else is coming near us, so we keep talking.

He nods. "She sure was; I wish I'd known her better. You were a close friend?"

"Not really, I'm sorry to say. A friend and I run a dog rescue organization called the Tara Foundation."

"Andy Carpenter . . . right. She told me all about you; I even looked you up. You're a big-time defense attorney."

"A big-time semiretired defense attorney, but that's not how I knew Rachel. She rescued a dog from us."

"I know. Lion. What a great dog . . . maybe the coolest dog I've ever been around."

"She wanted you to have him if anything happened to her. She asked me to step in if you didn't want him."

"Wow. I'd love him. I was wondering how to go about it. I had a dog, a Great Dane mix, but he died about three months ago. The house feels empty without a dog in it."

I'm glad to hear this; it sounds like Lion will have a good home.

There's no reason for me to be here anymore, but Bernie calls the session to order, so it feels awkward for me to get up and leave. Eight people are in the room, and that's including Bernie, Tony, and me.

Bernie welcomes everyone and expresses his condolences at the loss of Rachel Morehouse, though I don't know what relationship she had with any of these people. He no sooner starts reading the document than the door opens and a young woman enters.

Bernie looks up and says with a trace of annoyance, "What is it, Cynthia?"

She smiles nervously but doesn't answer. Instead she walks over to Bernie and hands him a piece of paper, which he reads. His face reveals his surprise, with some concern thrown in.

"I'm sorry, ladies and gentlemen, but there is going to be a bit of a delay. I'm afraid I have to ask you to step into the anteroom for a moment. All except Anthony Wasserman. Anthony, please remain in the room."

We get up and head toward the anteroom. I'm the last one in, and before I close the door behind us, I see four men walk into the conference room. I recognize one of them; he is Lieutenant James McDowell of the New Jersey State Police. Since we are not in New Jersey, I'm pretty sure that something unusual is going on.

Whatever it is, it happens quickly. We're let back in after less than ten minutes. When we return, Bernie is alone in the room with no sign of Tony. Bernie says that he regrets to inform us that the session will have to be postponed due to unforeseen events. A number of people question it, some aggressively, but he doesn't volunteer any more information.

I stay behind when the others leave. He notices that. "Andy, I really can't say anything."

"Tony has been arrested."

"How did you know that?"

"I have some experience in this area. What's the charge?"

He hesitates, then shrugs in resignation. "The murder of Rachel Morehouse."

I nod; I'm not surprised after seeing Lieutenant McDowell enter and then not seeing Tony Wasserman again. "That really is an unforeseen event. Do you know him? I mean, beyond this situation?"

"No, but I do know that Rachel seemed to care for him. Or at least she was hoping they could have a good relationship."

"Where did they take him?"

"Not sure, but he's going to wind up in Jersey because that's where she died. Local cops made the arrest, but a Jersey state cop was with them."

"Okay."

As I get ready to leave, Bernie says, "We'll reschedule this for next week."

"I'll make arrangements to get the dog on my own."

"That's not all she left you."

"Oh?"

"She left two million dollars to the Tara Foundation."

"Did you just say what I think you said?"

He nods. "Yes, sir. Two million dollars."

"Rachel obviously had good taste in foundations."

Two million dollars is a lot of money, but the Tara Foundation doesn't need any of it.

Willie Miller and I provide all the funding for the Foundation. I am independently wealthy, the result of a large inheritance and some lucrative cases.

Willie is pretty well off himself. He received $10 million for a civil case we filed after he was wrongly convicted for murder and spent seven years in prison. He has since invested the money wisely.

Running a dog rescue operation is not cheap, but we can handle it easily. Many groups are desperate for money; we are not one of them.

"So give the money to other rescue operations," Laurie says, when I tell her about the provision in the will.

"That's what I was thinking, but Rachel left the money to us, and I feel a little weird just passing it on."

"So keep it and donate your own money to other groups."

"It's our money."

"You have my vote."

"Let me think about it. The whole situation is bothering me."

She nods. "I can tell, but it's not the money that's doing it. It's her phone call to you." Laurie has a way of knowing what I'm thinking before I do.

"Right. She's had Lion for a while, and all of a sudden she decides to make arrangements for him if she dies. Then not long afterwards she is murdered."

"Quite a coincidence."

Laurie is a former police lieutenant and is currently part of my investigative team, whenever I take on a client. She shares my disbelief in coincidences.

The story of the murder and arrest is all over the news. The presence of huge money in a story is second only to sex in attracting media interest. And the arrest of a family member elevates that even more. This one is likely to be milked by the media for a long time, especially if it goes to trial.

The police are not revealing the cause of death, or in this case the means by which the murderer committed the crime. I'm guessing it was a poisoning of some sort, since Rachel was originally assumed to have died of natural causes. The coroner obviously must have detected something in the autopsy that pointed toward an intentional killing.

"Was the stepson a beneficiary of the will?" Laurie asks.

"I have to assume so because only the beneficiaries would have been present at the reading. But that doesn't speak to the amount he would have received; he could have been getting a token amount."

"Will that become publicly known?"

"Yes, absolutely."

"And if he's convicted of the crime, what happens to the money he would have received? He doesn't get it, right?"

I nod. "Correct. A person cannot benefit from another person's death if they are found to have had a hand in it. In fact, a conviction is not necessary. He could be found responsible in a civil proceeding, which has an even lower standard of proof."

She smiles. "You're very sexy when you're talking lawyer talk."

"I can't tell you how many women have told me that. It's one of the reasons I want to retire; I'm exhausted from being adored."

"I can imagine. When are you getting Lion?"

"Bernie is working on it; if I don't hear from him by tomorrow, I'll start calling to torture him."

"Where's Lion now?"

"Still at Rachel's; the housekeeper is taking care of him, but initially he'll have to go into the shelter system. Once we get him out of there, we'll start trying to find him a home."

"Will that be difficult?"

"Unfortunately, yes, because of his age and size. And chows are not the easiest dogs to place anyway. But it only takes one person to fall in love with him, like Rachel did."

"You're very sexy when you're talking animal rescue."

I smile. "I've got it all."

Mr. Carpenter, this is Tony Wasserman. I would be very grateful if you would meet with me."

The first thought that goes through my mind is that I should not have answered the phone. The caller ID had said "Private Caller," which should have set off warning bells.

The first thing I say is "I'm semiretired."

"I understand; you mentioned that at the lawyer's office. I'm just choosing to focus on the *semi* part."

"I'm not taking on clients, Tony."

"Then maybe you can give me some guidance. I'm a chemistry teacher from Indiana; the New Jersey criminal justice system is not exactly familiar territory."

I should just say no. I certainly want to say no, but I've never been great at saying no.

So instead I say nothing and he fills the void. "I basically have no money to pay you."

"Is that designed to make the job more appealing?"

"No, but I believe in being up-front."

"So do I. I'll come talk to you, but I am not interested in taking on a client. And that is vastly understating the case."

"I understand. Thank you."

I get off the phone and tell Laurie about the conversation. Her response is brief: "Uh-oh."

"What does that mean?"

"It means you might have gotten a client."

"It does not mean that at all. I specifically told him I was not interested in taking on a client." I turn to an imaginary person. "Court reporter, what exactly did Mr. Carpenter say? 'He said, "I am not interested in taking on a client."'"

She smiles. "Look, I love it when you work. You're a great lawyer, and though you say otherwise, it engages you and you're happy when you're doing it, even if you complain all the time. I just think that there's a chance you're jumping back in with this case. A pretty good chance."

"Earth to Laurie, come in please, come in please. I just had the court reporter read back what I said."

"I know you said that, and I know you believe it." She's already annoying me. "But I also know you. You will go talk to this guy, and if you like him, and more importantly if you think he might be innocent, then you will want to help him. It's what makes you who you are, and I love you for it. But it's in your DNA."

I shake my head. "Laziness is my dominant gene."

"Okay, whatever you say. Have a nice time at the jail."

If there was any chance that I was going to become Tony Wasserman's attorney, Laurie just ended it. There is no way I am going to give her the satisfaction of being right. Stubbornness and pride coexist with the laziness as my three leading genetic traits.

I take the twenty-five-minute drive to the Bergen County Jail in Hackensack. I've been here a number of times, but not nearly as often as I've been to the jail in Passaic County, where Paterson is. I am therefore not as familiar with the correctional officers that run the place, which is a positive because they haven't had as much opportunity to get to know and dislike me.

Even getting in to see Tony is complicated. I tell the reception person that I am his attorney, words that cause me to gag a bit. Unfortunately, they already have the public defender listed as his attorney, so it creates some bureaucratic chaos and results in its taking an hour and a half for me to actually be in a room with him. That is an hour and a half of my life that I will never get back.

After thanking me for coming, he gets right to the point. "Let me explain my situation. I'm a high school chemistry teacher in Evansville, Indiana. My father was Stanley Wasserman, but it's understating the case that our relationship was strained. He always considered me somewhere between a disappointment and a failure. Money was how he kept score, and I never had much interest in it.

"When my mother left him and took me to Indiana, he cut her off financially and me emotionally, though there was very little emotional tie left to cut. I met Rachel a few times and really liked her, but because my relationship with my father became nonexistent, I never really got to know her.

"Then my father died about a year and a half ago, and I thought that was that. But Rachel recently reached out to me. I came to visit, stayed with her, and we really hit it off. I was very happy about it. Then I came home one day and found her body, lying on the floor in the hallway outside the den. I called nine-one-one and the medics came. They said it appeared to be a heart attack.

"I was ready to head back to Indiana and was trying to figure out how to get the okay to take Lion with me. Then I got a call to come to the reading of the will, though I was not aware that I was in it; I don't know why I would be. You were there, so you know the rest."

It might well have been a prepared speech, but it was effective.

"Do you know how she died?" I ask.

"No."

"Or why they suspect you?"

"No idea. I mean, I was staying there, so I had access to her, but beyond that, I don't know."

"Have you met with the public defender that was assigned to you?"

"Yes. She seemed very nice, and knowledgeable. But I'm not going to lie; I've read about your career and many of your cases. They gave me access to a computer for two hours. I'd be crazy not to hope that you would take my case." Then, "Though I know what you said; you've been very up-front with me."

I can't take your case because then Laurie will be able to lord it over me is what I'm thinking, but fortunately don't say out loud.

I'm in a bind here. I like this guy, though I barely know him. But I also liked Rachel a lot, and I feel like if someone killed her, then she deserves to have the real killer put away, whether it's Tony or someone else.

Then, of course, the Laurie factor looms large. Thinking back to my law school days, I have always considered the overriding principle in our justice system to be that everyone is entitled to a competent defense, unless it will cause the attorney's wife to say, "I told you so."

So it's between helping to ensure that a potentially innocent man does not spend his life in prison, or winning a verbal battle with Laurie.

Six of one . . . half a dozen of the other.

think I came up with a creative way to handle this," I say to Laurie when I get home.

"Oh?" she asks, a smug, condescending question if ever I heard one.

"Yes. I said that I would temporarily . . . that's *temporarily* . . . act as his cocounsel . . . that's *co*counsel . . . with the public defender. That way I will have access to the discovery material and facts of the case, and it will help me decide what I should do. If I doubt his innocence, I bail out. Smart, huh?"

"Ingenious. So you have a client?"

"Temporarily. As cocounsel. Did I mention those things?"

"I believe you did. This is good news; I'm glad to hear it."

"You're not going to say 'I told you so'?"

"Why would I say that? This wasn't a contest. You want to make sure justice is done, and you're willing to use your considerable skill as a lawyer to make sure of it."

That was not the reaction I was expecting, and I'm not sure how to deal with it. "So now you're trying to demonstrate that you're more mature than me?"

"Can you think of a time when I wasn't more mature than you?"

I shrug. "Not off the top of my head."

She smiles. "Neither can I. Now get to work."

I've never been thrilled with the phrase *get to work.* By definition it implies a negative; if the work I was getting to was enjoyable, I wouldn't have to be told to get to it.

But she's right; perhaps the most important part of an investigation, maybe even more important than the trial itself, is the beginning. It sets the tone for all that is to follow. Of course, as far as my involvement in this case goes, it's possible that nothing will follow. It all depends on what I find.

After all, I'm just the temporary cocounsel.

I'm not even sure what I want to find. If my inclination is that Tony could be innocent, then I'm self-aware enough to know that I am going to be stuck with a client. My initial impression of him was favorable; I liked him, and I would want him to get the best defense possible. So in that regard I would want to find evidence that I think points to his innocence.

However, if he did it, then he should go down. And if it's not him, then at this point it's entirely possible that the real killer would get away with it. The police are sure that they have their man, so they're not out looking for any other suspects. That is a terrible outcome as well.

So . . . here goes.

My first call is to Joel Hirsch. Joel runs the Public Defender's office in Bergen County. If there is a list of noble professions, then public defender has to be up near the top. They've gone through almost twenty years of schooling and have decided to use what they've learned to take a job in which they are overworked, underpaid, and rarely successful.

They do this because they believe everyone is entitled to a good defense, so they stand up to a system stacked against their clients. Deep down they know that those clients are often . . . make that very often . . . guilty, but that is not the point. They can't let that be the point because in our system no one is guilty until it's proven.

I've met Joel a bunch of times, and we were even doubles partners a few years ago in a charity tennis tournament. We lost 6–1, 6–0, and the only reason we got one game is that our opponents were feeling charitable. I was particularly awful that day, and Joel, a much better player than me, could not carry me.

Joel's first words when he picks up the phone are "Andy Carpenter . . . or should I call you Mr. Double Fault?"

"The sun was in my eyes."

"We were indoors."

"The roof was in my eyes."

We chitchat a bit, then I tell him why I'm calling. "I want to come on board, temporarily, as cocounsel for Tony Wasserman."

"Temporary cocounsel. You sure you want to make that big a commitment? Why don't you start as 'temporary, for-the-moment, partial, not-really-involved cocounsel'?"

"You public defenders are a bitter, sarcastic group. Very unpleasant."

"Gee, Andy, I'm sorry. Now what the hell is going on?"

"I have a connection to Rachel Morehouse, and therefore Tony Wasserman, through my dog rescue foundation. So I want to look into it, and if I think there is a reasonable chance that Tony did not do this, then I would take him on as a client."

"You're a piece of work."

"Aww shucks. Enough about me."

I know Joel is not going to resist this; it would make him happy to get what is going to be a complicated, expensive, and time-sucking case off his workload.

"I'm obviously going to have to clear this with the client," he says.

"Of course. And for your information, I already have. He seems to covet the genius that is Andy Carpenter."

"That's because he's never seen you on a tennis court. We'll get the okay from Wasserman, and then when he signs off, we'll get you the discovery material we've received so far. Then you can send the decision down from Mount Olympus."

"Thanks. But the way I do it, white smoke means I am taking the case; black smoke means you're stuck with it. Any view you want to share on the case at this point?"

"He's innocent. All our clients are innocent."

"Then how come they're all in jail?"

"We're unlucky."

Usually I start a case by gathering our legal team together for a meeting. It's definitely too soon to do that right now; I want to get the lay of the land first.

But this time the land laying is going to have to wait, at least for a couple of hours, since I have something even more important to do.

I head down to the Passaic County Animal Shelter, a place I am all too familiar with. As is normal policy, Lion was taken into custody by the authorities and placed into the shelter system. I pulled some strings to make sure he went to Passaic County, even though he was living in Bergen County. Such is the long reach and power of Andy Carpenter.

Fred Brandenberger runs the shelter; he's a good man in a tough job. He does the best he can by the dogs and cats, but unfortunately the supply of abandoned animals is directly proportional to the stupidity of the people who owned them.

Before I even go inside to talk to Fred I walk around the back toward the kennels. This is where the Tara Foundation gets most of its dogs to place in homes, so I know my way around here quite well. At the end of the row of runs, on the right side, is Lion.

With every fiber of my being I hate seeing dogs in cages. It's a sad commentary, but it bothers me more than seeing humans in jail cells. In most cases the humans have made choices that resulted in their being there; the animals deserve no such blame.

Lion goes crazy when he sees me, jumping up and down and putting his paws up on the bars. I reach through to pet him for a while, then say, "You just wait here; don't go anywhere. I will be right back."

I start to walk away, hating the idea that he thought I was going to get him out and might now be starting to have his doubts. I walk quickly to Fred's office, and he brightens when he sees me. He knows my partner, Willie Miller, and I take dogs from him to place in good homes, so he definitely views us as the good guys.

"Andy, I didn't realize you were coming down today."

"Hey, Fred, I'm here to get Lion."

He immediately looks troubled. "Boy, was I sorry to see him wind up back here." This is where we got Lion in the first place. "What a great dog. But you know it's a legal situation, right?"

He's saying that he's obligated to keep Lion until the justice system works its way through the process. "Let's get him out here while we talk, okay, Fred? I sort of promised him just now, so he's expecting it."

Fred nods, grabs his keys, and goes out to get Lion. A minute later they are back here; a boy and his dog. Lion runs over and jumps on me, nearly knocking me over.

"He remembers you," Fred says, which may or may not be true. Lion is affectionate toward everyone.

"Yup. We hit it off. I need to get him out of here, Fred. We cannot put him back in that cage."

"I knew you were going to say that. But there are these rules, Andy, and . . ."

"Come on, we've done this before. I know the rules, you need to maintain control of him until the case is over. Which is fine.

You're crowded, no space for him, so you appoint me as your assistant. I answer to you. So I take him with your permission. I work for you, so if I have him, he's technically under your control. Problem solved."

I know Fred will give in because he wants what's best for Lion, and he also wants to keep me happy. The Tara Foundation can get its dogs from plenty of other shelters, and Fred wants to remain at the top of the list.

"And you won't place him until I say it's okay?" This amounts to a concession speech.

"My word as an officer of the court and as your trusty assistant." I turn toward Lion. "Come on, Lion, let's get the hell out of here." He actually stands up and starts walking toward the door; Lion is as smart as he is adorable.

He waits for me to open the door, though he could probably plow through it. I take him down to the Tara Foundation, where Willie Miller and his wife, Sondra, are waiting for us. It's a happy reunion; they spent a lot of time with Lion when he was here and fell in love with him. It's pretty hard not to love Lion.

"He's coming home with us," Sondra says. "Cash wants to see his old friend. But we'll bring Lion here during the day; last time he loved playing with the other dogs."

"Perfect." Lion spent a lot of time at their house when the Foundation had him and became buddies with Cash, Willie and Sondra's Lab mix. I'm glad to know Lion won't be confined here at the Foundation. Obviously the dogs are well treated here, but it is still not a home.

This part of the day went well; now it's time to go home and dig through the discovery materials that Joel Hirsch sent to me. I am far less looking forward to that than I was to freeing my friend Lion.

The prosecution has not turned over a great deal in discovery yet, but what is here is fairly compelling.

This is obviously not a surprise. The police wouldn't make an arrest if they didn't have evidence that they think provided at least probable cause; the judge wouldn't have signed the arrest warrant.

Even though they are obligated to hand over exculpatory evidence, that doesn't mean they have searched particularly hard for it. It's an adversary system; they take a position and try to make it as strong as they can. This is just the initial salvo, and it's reasonably impressive.

The autopsy is what turned this into a murder case. Rachel Morehouse's body had some bruises on her wrists that were not consistent with a fall, and a slight trace of a needle mark on her left arm. The EMT that was called to the house, and the doctor who pronounced her dead, could have missed these things, but they didn't.

So an autopsy was called for, even though in the case of an elderly woman apparently suffering an heart attack that is not always the case.

Additionally, the autopsy and Rachel's medical records showed that she had lung cancer, which likely would ultimately have killed her. She had apparently been on chemo, so the lung cancer was something she knew about and was treating.

She also had significant heart problems, for which she was taking medication. Rachel Morehouse was not a healthy woman.

The actual cause of death was a heavy concentration of potassium chloride, or KCl. It can cause a significant heart arrhythmia even in a healthy person, and at this level would almost certainly cause death in a person in Rachel's condition.

Trace levels on her arm proved that the chemical was administered by injection, and the coroner believed that the bruises on her wrists likely resulted from her being held down.

Tony, who was staying in the house, obviously had the opportunity to have done it. As a chemistry teacher, he also had the ability to create the drug. Most damning is that traces of KCl were found in his car and the bedroom he was staying in at Rachel's house.

A neighbor also overheard what she described as a loud argument between the two of them the morning of Rachel's death.

In total it is more than enough to have provided probable cause, and unfortunately also more than enough to get a jury to convict. Whether it will be sufficient to get me to bail out of the case remains to be seen. I'll have to have another talk with Tony first, and there's no time like the present.

This time I'm able to navigate the process at the jail more quickly since they know me from last time and now I am actually listed as one of Tony's lawyers. I'm going to have to decide soon whether to remove that listing, which is why I'm here.

"Have you made a decision?" Tony asks, clearly anxious.

I decide not to answer the question. Instead I say, "They found heavy traces of potassium chloride in Rachel's system."

"That's what killed her?"

"Could it?"

"Of course. She had a heart condition; she told me that. She was on blood thinners and cholesterol meds. Depending on how heavy the dose, potassium chloride would have stopped her heart for sure. So she was really murdered?"

"Unless she injected herself."

He shakes his head. "No way she would have done that."

Tony's openly admitted knowledge of the potential deadly effect of the drug, plus his downplaying the chance of her suicide, are positive marks for him on the Andy Carpenter report card.

"Would you know how to create potassium chloride?" I ask.

"You don't have to create it; you could just buy it. But, yes, if I had the raw elements, I could certainly create it."

"And you could adjust the strength?"

"For sure. Is that why they think it was me?"

"Partially. That and the traces of it that they found in your car and bedroom."

The shock on his face is obvious, and either real or fake. "That can't be."

"You sure?"

"I mean, I'm a chemist, so I work with various compounds, more as a hobby than anything else. So there could be chemical traces in my car, but not potassium. That's not possible. And definitely none in my room; I did not do any work at Rachel's house. It's ridiculous."

"That's what they found."

"Where?"

"In your car and bedroom."

"I mean, where in the car?"

"I believe it was in the trunk; I'm pretty sure that's what the forensics report showed."

He shakes his head vehemently. "No. No. That clinches it. I always kept any material in the front with me, just in case there was anything that could be volatile. Not that there often was, but it became force of habit. I never put chemicals of any kind in the trunk."

"So someone else put it there?"

"Either that, or they're wrong about it being there. Andy, my guess is that everyone you've ever spoken to in my situation has claimed to be innocent. I understand that. But this time it is true. I could never kill anyone, and I had no reason to hurt Rachel Morehouse. But if chemicals were really found where they said they found them, then someone put them there to incriminate me. There can't be any other explanation."

"Someone reported overhearing an argument between you and Rachel the morning she died."

He shakes his head. "Never happened; Rachel and I never argued . . . not once. And I wasn't home most of that morning."

"Where were you?"

"Running errands mostly. I took Lion with me and we went for a run in the park, and then went for coffee and a bagel." He smiles. "I had coffee and Lion had the bagel; he ate it in one big gulp."

I can easily see Lion doing just that. "Did Rachel ever talk to you about the contents of her will?"

"No. As I told you, I was surprised that I was in it when the lawyer called to tell me to come to the reading."

"Did she ever tell you that she was ill?"

"She told me about the heart condition, and I saw her take a lot of medication, so I assumed it was something significant. But it wasn't my place to ask questions. This was a nice lady; she deserved her privacy."

"She was incredibly rich."

"So that means she can't be nice?"

"That's not what I'm saying. In the big picture, the accumulation of money can be seen as a zero-sum game. If she had your father's money, it means that someone else didn't. People have been killed for a lot less."

"Not by me."

I nod. "Okay."

"Any chance that means 'Okay, I'll be your lawyer'?"

My head makes the decision for me, though without consulting the brain inside it.

My head nods up and down, rather than from side to side. "I'll be your lawyer."

find that walking the dogs gives me a chance to do my best thinking. It also gives me a perfect opportunity to berate myself when I've done something I regret.

This morning I will get to do both. I can yell at myself for taking on a client, while also preparing my first steps in the case. I've set a meeting with the team for later this morning, when we can kick it into gear.

The berating portion of my walk is surprisingly short. I am slowly and grudgingly coming to terms with the fact that I am a lawyer who practices law. It's my own fault; I should have realized this could happen when I went to law school.

The knot in the pit of my stomach is not because I will be facing an intense mountain of work, though I'm not thrilled about that. It's also not that it's going to cost me a lot of money. I didn't discuss a fee with Tony, because unless teachers in Indiana get paid far better than teachers everywhere else in the western hemisphere, he can't pay it.

If it turns out that Rachel left him her money, and if he gets acquitted and can therefore receive that money, he can pay my fee out of petty cash. If not, he can't. Either way, that's not what's worrying me.

Two things scare me, and it happens at the beginning of every case. I am scared that Tony committed the murder, and I'm scared that he didn't.

If he did, and I find that out during the trial, I could be responsible for letting a killer go free. I know that's how our system works, that everyone is entitled to a competent defense, but if someone is guilty, I'd much rather not be the provider of that competent defense.

But if he did not do it, and I can't prevent him from being convicted, that's even worse. He would likely languish in prison for the rest of his life, all because his lawyer wasn't good enough to get the jury to see the truth.

"Tara, why did you not talk me out of this?" I ask, but Tara doesn't answer. She's too busy sniffing, and she's a dog, so she can't talk anyway. But she can think, which she has demonstrated many times, and I'll bet right now she's thinking, *Don't blame me for this one, pal. You walked into it, eyes open.*

Just thinking about all this makes the knot in my stomach grow to the size of an average station wagon.

The way I deal with this kind of pressure is to just push ahead on the specifics of the case, one step at a time. It's not unlike how a professional athlete has to do it. A baseball player can't start the season thinking about the World Series; not if he wants to succeed. He has to take it one game, one inning, one at bat, at a time.

The first step is to gather the team, which we are doing this morning. I bring the dogs home, where Laurie and Ricky are waiting for me. Laurie, as an integral part of the team, will be coming to the meeting.

We're dropping Ricky off at his friend Will Rubenstein's house. Ricky is in that three-week window between the end of the school year and overnight camp. Will's father, Brian, owns a boat; it's a forty-one footer, as Brian precisely and invariably points out. They're going out on it today.

I don't get the whole boating thing. Owning a boat's an incredible amount of work, and Brian is always either working on it, or paying someone else to work on it. It seems as if there's about an hour and a half every year when nothing on the boat is broken, and usually it's raining that day.

But even on the rare occasions when the boat is functioning perfectly, I don't understand the appeal. I asked Brian what he and his family do on the boat that he enjoys so much, and he told me they relax and read and have lunch and feel the wind on their faces. They can even take the boat right up to a restaurant, though if they're having lunch on the boat, that seems like a lot of eating.

But the question I had but did not ask him was, Which of these things cannot be done on land? I relax and read and have lunch all the time just sitting in my recliner, and if I want a breeze, I have a ceiling fan I can use, or I can open a window. And while I'm doing those things, I never have to worry about hitting a rock and sinking. No one has ever drowned on my recliner; it's a record I am quite proud of.

It takes Brian and family two and a half hours to float to the same restaurant that I can drive to in twenty minutes, and there is no danger that seasickness will make me throw up the chicken parmigiana on the way home. Best of all, at the end of the summer, I don't have to pay someone to come get my recliner and store it for the winter, just so they can bring it back for more money to reinstall it in the spring.

My recliner has other advantages. For one, it's inside my house, so I don't have to travel to it. It's also positioned in front of a large flat-screen TV and within walking distance of the refrigerator. It doesn't depend on good weather for me to use it, and I never feel obligated to invite other people to share it. And I can make one phone call from my recliner and get a pizza delivered. Just try to do that when you're at sea; you'll wait forever.

But Ricky seems excited at the prospect of spending the day on the boat, so I see no reason to point out all the obvious deficiencies. Laurie and I drop him off, I admonish him not to take off his life jacket, and we head to my office.

We park in front of the fruit stand on Van Houten Street. The owner of the stand and building is Sofia Hernandez, so I rent the second-floor space from her. It's basically a dump, but it keeps me connected to my roots and to some of the best cantaloupes on the East Coast.

When we get out of the car, I look up toward the office and take a deep breath. The case is officially beginning now, and it will dominate everything until it resolves. It feels like I'm about to climb to the top of Mount Everest, and the fruit stand is base camp.

But this is what I do; I've come to terms with it.

I'm a lawyer.

A lazy lawyer, but a lawyer.

The team is assembled and waiting for us.

Most of them don't share my aversion to work; the only one who does, my assistant, Edna, is not here. She's getting married in November and spends twenty-four hours a day, every day, preparing for it.

Right now she and her fiancé are in the Caribbean scouting possible locations for a destination wedding. I'm not a big fan of weddings and have been spending my time trying to come up with an excuse not to go. I've got some ideas, but I obviously can't finalize them until they come up with a definite date.

The advantage of employing someone like Edna, who does absolutely no work when she's here, is that I don't have to find someone to fill in for her when she's not.

The conference room in my office, such as it is, is about the size of an average walk-in closet. The table is about a twentieth of the size of the one in Bernie Hudson's office, but it fills up most of this room, and everyone present sits with the back of their chair almost touching the wall.

Present are the usual suspects. The two other members of Laurie's "K Team" investigative unit sit nearest the window. They are Corey Douglas, like Laurie a former member of the Paterson Police Department, and Marcus Clark, the single toughest and scariest human I know.

Actually, there is another member of the K Team, Corey's police dog, Simon Garfunkel, but Simon is in my office room chewing on a rawhide bone. He apparently trusts Corey to relay any important information to him.

Eddie Dowd, the only other lawyer in the firm, sits next to Corey, and to his left is Sam Willis. Sam is my accountant, but his role here is as the cyber-detective in our group. Sam can hack into anything online, and since the entire history of the human race is online, that makes him a valuable source of information.

Sitting here, in a dumpy office above a fruit stand, the group would not strike fear into the heart of a legal adversary, and certainly not one with the legal resources of the State of New Jersey. But in fact we are a damn good team, and I'd pit us against anyone, even though I wish I didn't have to.

Laurie sits down next to Sam, but I remain standing, since I called the meeting. "Welcome, everyone." I then say the four words I always dread saying: "We have a client."

This does not come as a shock to anyone; they all knew they weren't called here for a book-club meeting. So they just wait to hear who it is we are defending and what the circumstances are.

"His name is Tony Wasserman, and he's accused of the homicide of Rachel Morehouse, who happened to be his stepmother. I'm sure most of you have read about it since it's been prominent in the media, but Rachel was a billionaire, and a friend of mine."

I continue with the little I know about the case from the discovery. I don't comment on whether or not I consider Tony to be innocent. I don't have a formed view on that yet, and the truth is, it's not relevant. We will do the best we can for him; that is our commitment, and that is what the system calls for.

"I don't know this for a fact yet, but I feel comfortable saying that this case is ultimately going to be about money. Rachel had it, someone else wanted it, and they were willing to kill for it.

"So we have to find out who was going to profit from her death, and how that was going to happen. That shouldn't be so hard to do, but proving that person killed her will likely turn out to be the tough part.

"Corey, Marcus, and Laurie, you can start digging into that right away. Sam, get online and find out everything you can about Wasserman Equities. Rachel had the controlling interest in it. It's a multibillion-dollar firm, with a great many financial interests, so it will be complicated. The sooner you can come up with at least the idiot's guide to it, the sooner we'll have a road map to follow.

"Eddie, there's not much for you to do right now. The public defender handled the arraignment, and Tony pled not guilty. The prosecutor is Kathryn Strickland. She's new to the department, so I don't know much about her. She moved up here from Delaware and has a pretty good reputation. See what you can find out about her.

"You might as well prepare a motion to request bail. It was denied at the arraignment and will be denied again, but it can't hurt to try. Any questions?"

Corey asks, "Do we have a copy of the will?"

"Not yet, but we will soon. I don't know how Tony fits into that, though I know he was at least a beneficiary in some fashion. Obviously, the list of other beneficiaries will be important. I was one of them; the Tara Foundation was left two million dollars.

"But I didn't murder Rachel Morehouse, and neither did Tara. So you can cross both of us off your list of suspects."

I adjourn the meeting. We will have a great deal to do, and

not a lot of time to do it in, but at this point we're just feeling our way around.

I drop Laurie off at home and head for Manhattan. Since the case is about money, I'm going to get a crash course in it.

obbie Divine collects money the way other people collect stamps or baseball cards.

Accumulating money is his job, his life's work, and he's good at it. I once asked him how much he had, and his answer expressed his frustration at not being able to accurately answer the question. He was constantly increasing his wealth, literally by the minute, so there was no way to finish counting.

Robbie is an investor. He doesn't own any companies, at least not officially, and therefore he doesn't create anything other than wealth. He sends his money out every morning with instructions to bring home some friends.

He is different than Stanley Wasserman was in that regard, in that Wasserman bought controlling interests in companies and then picked people to run them.

"I bet on people," Robbie once told me. "I don't care very much what they do or what they make. That's within reason; I mean I wouldn't invest in cigarettes, or terrorists. I pick people that are smart, and I put my money on them. I make sure that my economic interests align with theirs, so when they do well, I do well. And the people I bet on almost always do well."

It seems strange to say, but even though Robbie spends all his time accumulating money, he's not greedy. He supports many charitable causes with generous donations; we even met for the first time at a dinner supporting some worthy cause, though I don't remember which one.

The money he makes doesn't change his lifestyle any; he couldn't spend it all if he tried. It's just the way he amuses himself.

I've gone to Robbie a bunch of times to take advantage of his expertise on financial matters. He's always been generous with his time. All I have to do is say something nice about the Chicago Cubs, his other passion in life.

Typically, Robbie agreed to make time for me when I called him yesterday, so I'm heading into Manhattan to meet him at his office on Thirty-sixth and Park. I've been here before, and today I'm again struck by how unpretentious it is. It's not above a fruit stand, but it's almost as unimpressive as my office. Robbie doesn't care about trappings; it's one of the things I like about him.

In my experience, only one other employee works here. Her name is Maureen and I guess she's his assistant. She is unfailingly upbeat but never seems to have anything to do. Edna would do great at this job.

Robbie sits behind his desk wearing his Chicago Cubs baseball hat. The season has not started well for the Cubs; when I checked the standings this morning, they were already six games below .500.

"Tough season so far. But they'll turn it around." I say this even though I know they won't be getting any better; with their current lineup they'd have a tough time beating Ricky's team.

Robbie shakes his head. "No, they won't. They can't pitch and they can't score. Tough to win games that way. Makes me nauseous."

"You're right." I nod. "They stink."

"Hey, watch it. That's my team you're talking about."

I nod again, agreeably. "And a damn good team they are."

"What are you talking about? They're awful. Now, what the hell are you doing here?"

"I'm representing the person accused of killing Rachel Morehouse."

"Wasserman's wife?"

"Yes."

"Nice lady. I have no idea why she married that asshole."

"You were not a fan of Mr. Wasserman?"

"What tipped you off?"

"I can just sense things; it's a gift. Why didn't you like him?"

"Because I knew him; nobody who knew him liked him."

"Rachel Morehouse must have; she married him," I say.

"I know. I could never see them together. But there's no accounting for taste."

"Tell me about his business."

Robbie frowns his distaste. "His business was buying businesses. He'd target a company, buy it, and then install his own managers. Stupid way to operate."

"Why is that stupid?"

"Because when you buy a business, you're buying the people that run it. Change those people and you change the business. Now sometimes that can make sense; you can take over a business you think is vastly underachieving, get it at a good price, and run it better. But not Wasserman; he was all about control. Hence, stupid."

"What kind of businesses did he buy?"

"What am I, your research director? This information is readily available."

"I know, but I come to you because you're smart and knowledgeable."

He frowns again. "You're full of shit, but in this case accurate. . . . The kind of businesses he bought was another reason he was stupid. He bought all different kinds, mostly unrelated to each other."

"So?"

"So a person in his position should have an area of expertise to focus on. You're a criminal attorney. Do you also handle divorces, insurance litigation, and antitrust law?"

"God forbid."

"Exactly."

"Where did Wasserman get his money to make all these purchases?"

"Good question; he just seemed to appear on the scene. Then for a while he was in trouble; that was a while ago when the economy tanked. But he survived; maybe he raised the money from investors that were dumb enough to trust him."

"But you don't know who those investors are?"

"I don't want to know."

"What does that mean?"

"Next question." Robbie obviously wants no part of the one on the table.

So I try a different one. "And now? With him gone, and with Rachel gone, what happens to Wasserman Equities?"

"I'm sure it will go on. Stanley wasn't the only person there; he had two guys running it for him. They are smarter than he was, but then again this desk is smarter than he was."

"Can you get me in to see them?"

"What am I, your admin?"

"What kind of a salary would you require? And would you be willing to get me coffee and call me Mr. Carpenter?"

"Not in this lifetime. . . . Yeah, I can get you in to see them. I can get you in to see anyone."

I smile. "That's one of the many things I like about you. . . . Who are the Cubs playing today?" I ask, having exhausted the Wasserman subject.

"What's the difference? They stink."

"Before, when I said they stink, you jumped on me. Now you're saying it yourself?"

He nods. "Right. I can say it because they're family. You're an outsider."

This is my second time attending a reading of Rachel Morehouse's will.

It brings the total of will readings I have attended in my life to two. My father, when he passed away, left everything to me, so there was no reason to have a formal reading. Our lawyer simply told me about it and gave me a copy.

That turned out to be fairly eventful because my father left me $22 million that I never knew he had, but that's another story.

Probably twice as many people are here today in Bernie's conference room as there were last time. Obviously some beneficiaries hadn't felt the need to be present during the initial reading, but this has now become a media event. They missed a murder arrest last time, so they want to be present for any surprises or excitement today.

Fortunately, this room would not feel overcrowded if the organizers of the Million Man March decided to hold their reunion here, so there's not exactly a need to rush and grab a seat.

The media has gathered in force downstairs to cover the gathering and interview us when we leave. A few of them recognized me going in and fired off their questions about Tony's defense, but I ignored them. I'll be just as talkative on the way out.

I'm not opposed to talking to the press, but only when I have a public message to convey on behalf of my client. I don't have that yet, so I'll keep my mouth shut.

Soon there will be speculation about how the Tara Foundation's receiving $2 million represents some kind of conflict of interest with my defending Tony, but I'll be able to fend that off.

I don't see where it raises any serious legal issues, and for public relations purposes it probably works in our favor. My position will be that Rachel was obviously a friend, so why would I not want to find her killer? And why would I represent someone that did the deed?

I don't see any members of the prosecution here today, though it's possible that they sent a member of the team that I don't recognize. I don't know whether they already know what's in the will, most particularly what Tony was supposed to get or not get. They don't have to prove motive, so it might not be in the discovery at this point.

The bottom line is that they can easily accommodate their view of the case to whatever is in the will. If Tony is supposed to get a fortune, they can claim that he wanted Rachel dead so that he could collect it immediately and start spending it.

If he is shut out or close to shut out, they will just say that he found out about it, was furious, and killed her to exact his revenge.

Like last time, everyone has a somber expression, in keeping with the fact that someone died. I have no idea which ones knew Rachel well or cared for her, and which ones are here because they are hoping to reap the rewards of her death. But whatever one's point of view, this is not the kind of event where you want to look gleeful.

Bernie, for his part, handles the situation with professionalism. He calls the session to order and again explains why we are gathered. You would never know by his manner that this has become something far from the ordinary; you wouldn't even know that this is the second attempt at getting through it.

He gets past the part where he was interrupted by the police coming in to arrest Tony and finally actually reads the will. I am mentioned as the person to take care of Lion, who she describes as her "beloved companion," and as the head of the Tara Foundation, to which she left $2 million.

Tony is mentioned once. He was to receive $300,000, as specified in Stanley Wasserman's will. He had said that the money should go to Tony upon Rachel's death. It is a paltry sum considering his vast wealth; the father obviously had some significant issues with the son.

Tony had told me about their strained relationship, so I'm not particularly surprised by it. But the prosecution will have no problem claiming that Tony was pissed off at being almost completely shut out of an estate worth billions.

No reference is made to Tony taking possession of Lion; I assume Rachel was waiting to hear his response to her request. I'm listed probably because Rachel knew I wouldn't refuse. Actually, the standard terms of the Tara Foundation's adoption agreement require a dog to be returned to us if for any reason the owner cannot keep him or doesn't want to.

Sums of money, substantial but not enormous, go to people I don't know, so I have no idea if they are family of either Rachel's or Stanley Wasserman's. The majority of Rachel's estate, which is the holdings in Wasserman Equities, will go into a trust to be formed to do charitable work. Her interests in the firm will be sold to provide the funding for the trust.

The named trustees will choose who will run the charitable foundation. Unfortunately, I am one of three of those named trustees, which means more work for me. This will is a gift that keeps on giving.

A reference is made to another document that talks about the way the sale will be structured, but fortunately Bernie does not read it. He does say that the current co-CEOs, James Wolford and Carl Simmons, will have the first opportunity to buy the company.

When it's over, everyone leaves, with most of them looking somewhere between disgruntled and outright pissed off. That Rachel left almost all of her money to a charitable foundation has seemed to make these people less charitable. I get up as well, but Bernie says, "Andy, can you stay a minute?"

"Sure."

Once the room is empty, Bernie says, "This is not really in my area of expertise, so I'm thinking you would be a good person to ask."

"Shoot."

"There was a conversation that Rachel and I had that might be relevant to the case. I can't reveal it because it's privileged, but I'm wondering if there is a way around that."

"If it's helpful to my client, there's definitely a way around it. If it goes against his interests, you'll have to take it to the grave."

He smiles, though I doubt he thought my comment was particularly funny. "I knew I could count on you. The truth is I have no idea which way it would cut, or if it would be of any consequence at all. It might be."

I nod. "Okay. Not sure I have all that much experience at this either. But if I were you, I would go to the court handling this case, tell the judge what you told me, and he would be able to release you from the privilege. That's if he feels he should."

"Who is the judge?"

"Sidney Lofton . . . Bergen County Court. I'm not very familiar with him, but he has a good reputation."

"Okay. Thanks, Andy."

"No problem. By the way, I'd like the two million in small, unmarked bills."

He smiles again. "I'll take care of it."

On every case, Laurie and I always visit the murder scene. Sometimes that brings us to dingy, dirty, depressing areas.

This isn't one of those times.

The scene is believed to be Rachel's house in Upper Saddle River, since that's where the body was found. So Laurie and I have come here, though there isn't terribly much to be learned.

There is still a police presence here, though I cannot imagine that any forensics information remains to be obtained. I had called the prosecutor on the case, Kathryn Strickland, to clear the way for our being allowed in, and she was pleasant and accommodating. Clearly she has not read the prosecutorial handbook, which dictates making things as difficult as possible for the defense.

The house sits on eleven acres of the most expensive real estate in New Jersey. I can't say that it fits the neighborhood because, with no other homes in sight, it is the entire neighborhood.

We park around back at the end of the seemingly endless driveway, since that is where two police cars are parked. From here we can see the pool, which is so large that Michael Phelps would probably have to rest before completing a full lap.

Beyond the pool are two tennis courts, one hard court and one clay. I suppose Stanley and Rachel would decide which one to play on depending on whether they were training for the US or French Open.

We walk around the house to the front. The door is unlocked; I guess the police presence is considered a substantial enough deterrence to potential invaders.

"Lion was living the high life," Laurie says as we enter, and I know what she means. The foyer is enormous; I can just see Lion running around in it. Actually, it's big enough that I can see the Knicks running around in it.

It's obvious where the body was found since two cops are guarding the door to the area. I wave to them, but get no response. Fortunately they must have been notified that we were coming because they haven't drawn their weapons and threatened to shoot us.

Laurie wants to walk around and check out the house. It's spectacular; every piece of furniture and art has obviously been chosen with great care. It's all very formal, which makes it hilarious to picture Lion in this place. It's actually hard to picture Rachel Morehouse here as well; she seemed completely casual and unpretentious.

I hope Laurie's not thinking of making an offer on the place, since with all the residents now deceased, I would assume it would go on the market. We're rich, but we probably couldn't afford to purchase one of the bathrooms. On the positive side, if we moved in here, Tara, Sebastian, and Hunter could all have their own room.

One of the bedrooms we enter has men's clothing and possessions in it, so this is probably where Tony was staying. It's also where trace levels of potassium chloride were discovered. The room is far from Rachel's bedroom; everything in this house is far from everything else.

We work our way back to where the two cops are and tell them that we need to look around. One of them says, "No problem," and they step aside. If all they do is stand here all day and guard this door, our arrival on the scene is probably pretty damn exciting.

We go through the door, which leads to a large hallway. We see absolutely nothing of any consequence. The area where the body must have been discovered is roped off, but there is no chalk outline of the body. This wasn't even considered a murder scene for a couple of weeks after Rachel's death; she was just considered to be a heart attack victim.

According to the forensics, nothing of value was gathered from the scene itself. I'm not surprised; based on the immaculate condition of this place, the housekeeper must have cleaned the area thirty-eight times in the intervening two weeks.

It's interesting to me that the discovery showed traces of potassium chloride in the room where Tony was staying; I make a mental note to ask the housekeeper if she cleaned it regularly; if the answer is yes, it might help us to claim that the chemical was placed there later on.

"If they had known it was a murder, the scene could have told us something," Laurie says. "Not a lot, but something."

"What do you mean?"

"Would the potassium chloride injection have killed her quickly?"

"Apparently so, at the levels in her blood."

"Then she was accosted in this hallway, forced to the floor, and injected with the chemical. We would at least know which doors to this hallway were open, which might tell us where the killer came from. There might have been some marks on the floor, something that would indicate what kind of shoes he was wearing, or if there was a struggle. Most importantly, the killer might have left DNA. None of that was possible to detect two weeks later, not in this environment."

"One other thing bothers me," I say. "And that's the position of the house itself."

"How so?"

"This is not a house you sneak up on. You can't just drive up that driveway undetected, and it seems unlikely the killer would park at the bottom and walk. There is too much chance that someone would notice something unusual."

"Which means that Rachel either let the killer in or knew he was here?"

"That's what I would argue if I was the prosecution. It's an easy case for them to make."

"Where was the housekeeper at the time?"

"It was her day off," I say. "So this took planning and knowledge of the housekeeper's work schedule, which is another inconvenient fact to deal with."

"What is Tony's esteemed counsel going to come up with to counter it?"

"That is an excellent question."

Lorraine Baumann was Rachel's housekeeper. Lorraine has agreed to talk to me at her house in Suffern, New York.

Suffern is right across from New Jersey on Route 17; the nearest town in Jersey is Mahwah. The modest house is in what seems like a working-class neighborhood. It's five miles and 5 million light-years away from the house where Lorraine went to work every day.

As soon as Lorraine comes to the door, I recognize her from the will reading. She was crying softly before, during, and after the reading, and the fact that Rachel left her $5 million seemed to have little effect on her emotions.

Rachel obviously cared about her, and unless Lorraine is a great actress, the feelings were reciprocated.

She greets me with a sad smile at the door and invites me in. We go into her kitchen, where I accept her offer of coffee but I decline some great-looking blueberry muffins. I got a quick look at the mirror in the bathroom this morning, and it was as if someone wrote in large letters, *You might want to cut back on the muffins, Carpenter.*

"Thanks for seeing me." I had been surprised she was so willing, since in her view I'm probably representing the killer of her employer and friend.

"Ms. Morehouse spoke to me about you; she liked you. You

gave her Lion. And I saw you at the lawyer's office. So if Ms. Morehouse liked you, then . . ."

"You called her Ms. Morehouse?"

Lorraine smiles. "No, I called her Rachel. She insisted on it."

"She was a good person to work for?"

"She was a good person, period."

"Did you work there when her husband was alive?"

"Oh, yes. I was there for eight years."

"You saw Tony Wasserman and Rachel together?"

She nods. "Oh, yes; it made Rachel very happy. She had no other family, and she was afraid that Tony would not want a relationship with her because of the way things had been with his father."

"So they seemed to get along?"

"Very well."

"You were surprised when the arrest was made?"

"Yes. I was shocked."

"Did you clean Tony's room regularly?"

She shakes her head. "No, he said he would do it himself, that he didn't want to impose."

"So you never cleaned his room in the time after Rachel died?"

"No."

This is disappointing to hear. Had she cleaned it, I could have challenged when the trace potassium chloride was deposited there. "Can you think of anyone who might have wanted to kill Rachel?"

She thinks for a few moments. "No, everyone loved her." Then, "But when there is so much money . . ."

"You knew she was ill?"

Lorraine nods sadly. "Oh, yes. Poor Rachel was suffering, the treatments took so much out of her. But she never complained. She had such courage, and she never gave up."

"So you don't think she could have taken her own life?"

An emphatic shake of the head. "Absolutely not. That was not her way. I would never believe she would do that."

"I need a road map, which you might be able to provide. If you could give me a list of her friends, people that she liked and didn't like. People she might have confided in."

"I can do that. But understand that Rachel and I didn't hang out together; there would be much about her life that I wouldn't know."

"I do understand. But you know much more than I do, so that would be very helpful. And what about Stanley Wasserman?"

Lorraine's expression changes to what seems like wariness. "What about him?"

"Did you know him well?"

"No. I'm not sure anyone did. But he was nice to Rachel."

"Was he also an employer and a friend?"

She answers carefully, "He was my employer." Then, "I'll make up the list as best I can."

She goes off to get a pen and paper, giving me a chance to grab one of the blueberry muffins. Mirrors are known liars.

T hanks for coming in, Andy," Kathryn Strickland says.

"No problem. I was just worried I wouldn't dress right for a fancy Bergen County meeting. I'm used to Passaic."

She laughs an outstanding laugh. She comes across as pleasant and engaging, not exactly the norm for prosecutors who deal with me. "You did fine. I particularly like the sneakers. Defense attorney chic."

"Exactly. You obviously understand fashion. So what are we meeting about?" I ask, even though I know full well why we are meeting.

"I must say, I never expected that the first case I tried up here would be opposite Andy Carpenter."

"It doesn't have to be; you could dismiss the charges."

"That I can't do. I just hope you're not as good as your reputation."

"Come on, enough about me." I have no idea why she is praising me; she clearly is playing the stronger hand right now and doesn't need me for anything.

Her expression turns serious. "You obviously know how this works. I have been empowered to offer you a plea bargain, which you can accept or reject. But it is not negotiable from our end; our first offer is our best one."

"I'm hanging on your every word."

"Forty years. Possibility of parole after twenty-five." When I don't say anything, she adds, "It's a good deal, Andy."

"You don't think I know that? I'm just sitting here wishing I was the one in custody so I could grab that deal for myself."

"It's better than I would have offered if I was calling the shots. He acted coldly and with premeditation to take the life of a woman who was befriending him."

"Actually, he didn't. I say he is innocent, and unless and until you prove otherwise, so does the State of New Jersey."

"You've seen the discovery. Proving otherwise will not be a difficult task."

"Then go for it." I stand up.

"So you're turning down the deal?"

"No. I'll discuss it with my client. But taking a wild guess, I don't think he is going to want to spend most or all of the rest of his life in prison for a crime he did not commit."

"Fair enough. How about if we leave it that the offer remains on the table for forty-eight hours?"

I nod. "Sounds like a plan."

"It was nice meeting you, Andy. I guess the next time we'll meet will probably be in court?"

"I'll be wearing my dress sneakers."

She offers her hand and I shake it. "I had heard that you were retired."

"I heard the same thing," I say wistfully. "Someday it might even be true."

When I leave Strickland's office, I head down to the Tara Foundation. It always simultaneously cheers me up and depresses me to be there. I'm happy that we are able to care for and place so many dogs in great homes, but I'm sorry that they had to wind up there in the first place, and I know how many there are that we can't save.

But I'm here to check on Lion, and as soon as I walk in the door, I see how great he is doing. He's in the play area, wrestling with a dog about half his size. The other dog is dominating; it's nice of Lion to let him win.

Lion sees me, runs over to get petted, then heads back into the fray. The smile on Lion's face is extremely nice to see.

Tony will be getting a great dog.

I hope.

According to the Austrian passport, the man landing at JFK was named Wiktor Kowalski.

He was forty-one years old, six feet one and 220 pounds, and was born in Kraków. He told the customs agent that he was visiting his daughter and her family in New Jersey.

He proudly said that he was so happy to be in the United States because that daughter had just made him a grandfather. The agent was afraid Kowalski was going to start showing him photos of the newborn and thus quickly stamped the passport and told him to move on.

Wiktor Kowalski's story had a few minor inaccuracies. For one thing, his real name was not Wiktor Kowalski. The visitor went by the name Stal, which is Russian for "steel." When he was eighteen, he worked in a steel mill, as his father and three generations before him had done.

By the time Stal was nineteen, he had decided to pursue a more lucrative path. But the nickname seemed to fit him, so he kept it. He also found it was intimidating to people, and intimidation became Stal's go-to technique.

The truth was that no one besides Stal knew his real name, and that was the way he preferred it.

There were other inaccuracies in the passport and Stal's conversation with the customs agent. Stal was not Polish; he was

Russian. He was not forty-one; he was thirty-six. He was not visiting his daughter; he had no children, and certainly no grandchildren.

And he was certainly not happy to be in the United States. Stal was never happy to travel because he only did so when a situation had to be addressed.

The operation in the United States, as difficult as it had been to set up, had been running smoothly now for quite a while. But now there was the potential for trouble. It might resolve itself, and then Wiktor Kowalski could simply fly back home. But it could go the other way and become a serious problem. Then he would get involved.

Stal was, above all else, a problem solver.

James Wolford is one of the two Wasserman Equities executives that worked directly for Stanley Wasserman, and then for Rachel Morehouse when she took over.

He's one of the people that Robbie Divine promised to get me in to see, and I would think that would happen fairly soon.

In the meantime, I didn't need anyone to arrange a meeting with his wife, Susan Wolford. I simply called her and she showed no hesitation whatsoever; I didn't even have to turn on the famed Carpenter charm.

My interest in talking to Susan Wolford is not because of her husband's position, though that is a plus. Rather it is because Rachel's housekeeper, Lorraine Baumann, listed Susan as one of the people that would occasionally visit Rachel.

Her house is in Millburn, not far from the company headquarters in Montclair. It's a beautiful home; not quite at the level of Rachel's, but the Vatican is not quite at the level of Rachel's. Suffice it to say that no one is going to pull up to the Wolford house and decide to start a GoFundMe pitch to help them out.

A butler answers the door when I ring the bell. I'm assuming he's a butler, even though I haven't been around that many. He doesn't wear a tag saying BUTLER, and he doesn't introduce himself as Jeeves. But he does say butler kind of stuff, like "Welcome to the Wolford residence" and "Ms. Wolford is waiting for you in the sitting room."

"Is there also a standing room? Or a crouching room?" I ask, but the butler doesn't seem to consider that worthy of a reply.

He leads the way to the sitting room, which proves to be inaccurately named, since Susan Wolford is standing when I arrive. She walks over to shake my hand, but then goes and sits back down.

I sit as well, in deference to the name of the room, although the truth is I would probably have done the same thing if this was called the den.

I address her as Ms. Wolford, but she insists I call her Susan. I tell her to call me Andy, which officially puts us on a first-name basis. I turn down her offer of tea, even though I think that's probably what you drink in sitting rooms; you balance it on your lap and drink it with pinkie extended. Unfortunately, I hate tea of all kinds in all rooms.

"As I told you on the phone, I'm representing Tony Wasserman."

"Yes. Such a terrible, terrible situation."

"It certainly is. Right now I'm just doing background work, trying to learn who the various people were in Rachel's life. I understand you and she were close friends?"

"Oh, yes. I loved Rachel; everybody loved Rachel. She was a wonderful person. I still can't believe she's gone."

I refrain from saying that apparently not everybody loved Rachel, since someone obviously murdered her. "How did you two meet?"

"Through Stanley. Jim, that's my husband, worked with Stanley for years. Then when Stanley met and married Rachel, we just naturally became close."

"She was considerably older than you."

Susan smiles. "Thank you, but there wasn't as big an age difference as you might think. And Rachel's mind was youthful and fun."

"When her husband died, she effectively became your husband's boss?"

"I suppose that's true, but that company has always been a collaboration. And Rachel realized she knew very little about the business, so I'm sure she deferred to Jim and Carl quite a bit."

The Carl she is referring to is Carl Simmons, the other top executive at the company.

"Did you get to meet Tony Wasserman?"

She nods. "I did, a couple of times, at Rachel's. We didn't get to talk much, but he seemed nice enough. Not like how Stanley used to describe him."

"How was that?"

"Well, he didn't talk about him much, but he thought that Tony was unfocused, difficult to reach, always trying to find himself but never succeeding. I think Stanley was just disappointed that Tony did not share any of his interests."

"Like money?"

"You make it sound like a bad thing. Money can come in very handy."

"Was it important to Rachel?"

"I think it was, but in a different way than Stanley. Rachel was into philanthropy; she wanted to use the money in that way. I used to laugh and say that she was going to be a sucker for every charity that would come along."

"Do you know anyone who might have wanted to hurt her?"

"No. My goodness, I hope that Tony did not do what they say he did."

"You can rest easy, because he didn't. When was the last time you saw Rachel?"

"The morning she died. We had coffee at her house; she seemed fine physically, though a little sad. Things with Tony were not going as well as she had hoped."

I'm surprised to hear this and not pleased. "Do you know what was going on?"

"Not really. She didn't talk much about it. But I think the problem was still Stanley. Tony saw her as an extension of him. Stanley cast a long shadow, even after he was gone. He still does."

"How so?"

"Mostly through the business. He was a visionary, and to some degree Jim and Carl are still following that vision."

"Did Rachel ever mention anything about her will?"

"Not to me. I knew she had made arrangements because . . ." Susan hesitates, as if not sure whether to continue. Then, ". . . Rachel was quite ill."

"She openly talked about it?"

"Yes, at least to me. I should tell you, I used to be a nurse, before I got married. So Rachel would sometimes talk to me about health issues. And she knew I would respect her privacy. She was not giving up, but she was prepared to accept what might be coming."

"What did you and she talk about that last morning?"

"I'm not sure if I should say . . . it was personal."

"It could be important."

"I think she was just confronting the possibility that the disease could beat her, no matter how hard she fought. She was very happy about the state of the business; she felt it was in excellent hands. And she was glad her money would be used for good after she was gone. But she was sad about how things were with Tony."

"Did she seem afraid of anything?"

"No. Rachel was not the fearful type."

T he belief is that Stanley Wasserman was involved with dirty money," Corey Douglas says.

He and Laurie have done some preliminary investigating, as has Sam Willis in the online world. We're all at my house so they can update me on what they've learned.

"Dirty how?" I know it is a stupid question before the words fully pass my lips out into the hearing world. Sometimes I ask stupid questions to elicit certain responses, and sometimes I just ask them stupidly. In this case the latter applies.

Corey gives me a slight look of disdain. "Dirty like from people who don't want anyone to know where they got it because they didn't get it by working nine to five."

"Do we know who those people are in this case?"

Corey shakes his head. "We do not. Nor do we know if they are still involved with Wasserman Equities; it's quite possible they are not."

"Why would they have picked Stanley Wasserman to invest in?"

Laurie answers me this time. "Because he represented the perfect laundry for them. They had all this money; having Wasserman utilize it to buy businesses enabled them to move it into the legitimate world. And he wasn't buying mom-and-pop operations; these were substantial businesses that did not come cheap."

"And Wasserman didn't have to report where he got the money?"

"No, Wasserman Equities is a private enterprise, so the reporting requirements that a public company would have don't exist."

"Can I ask where you got this information?"

"You can ask, but . . ." Corey hesitates, then seems to change his mind. "I have a friend at the SEC that owed me a favor."

"Keep in mind, not only can't we prove this, but we can't say for sure that it isn't just speculation," Laurie says. "And even if it is true, it doesn't mean that it's ongoing."

Corey adds, "And at this point we certainly have no reason to tie it to the death of Rachel Morehouse."

I nod. "Okay, but just for argument's sake, let's say that whoever put this dirty money in was afraid that Rachel was going to kill the golden goose. They would have reason to get rid of her."

Corey shakes his head. "That's not how it would work. That money is already embedded there, it would have been there for years. The mechanics of it, and the cash flow, would have been part of the process. It's hard to imagine that Rachel, unless she was incredibly sophisticated, would have spotted it. It's not like mobsters show up to work there each morning and punch a clock.

"But there is always the possibility that she has known about it for years. She was married to Stanley the whole time."

I have trouble picturing that, but the truth is that I didn't know Rachel all that well. I didn't even know she was rich; all I knew was that she liked dogs and loved Lion.

The picture Corey is painting fits well with Robbie Divine's refusal to answer when I asked him where Wasserman's money came from. I doubt Robbie had the facts, so he probably didn't want to offer any information that he couldn't verify.

I turn to Sam, who has been quiet all this time. "What have you got?"

"Nothing nearly as juicy as that. I've just been looking at Wasserman Equities and how they operate. They're actually a small company in terms of personnel; as the parent company they have only eighteen employees.

"They currently own thirty-one companies. Over the last three years that number has held between twenty-eight and thirty-three. But the list has not stayed the same; they've sold seven companies in that time and bought eight. In most cases they buy them and turn them over pretty fast."

"What kind of companies?"

"They're all over the lot, and some are overseas. Shipping, private airlines, manufacturing, pharmaceutical, a headhunter job-placement firm, fast food . . . I've printed out a list for you to have. There's a core nine companies that they've had for almost eight years; I've indicated them on the list as well."

This is also consistent with what Robbie told me; that they have no coherent business model or particular expertise. He was disdainful of that approach.

"Is there any way for you to trace the source of Wasserman's money, back to when he started?"

Sam shakes his head. "Sorry, I wish there was. But that goes way back, and it's not like it would be transparent. Al Capone's name won't be on there; it would probably just be a series of shell companies."

"What about the companies they own? Can you take a look at them?"

"What am I looking for?"

That is a perfectly reasonable question. I wish I had a good answer for it. "I'm not sure, but I'll know it when you see it. Just irregularities of any kind."

"Thirty-one companies?"

"Can you bring in the Bubeleh Brigade?" Sam used to teach a senior class in computers at the YMHA, and he had a few terrific students that we have used to help him on some cases. They're smart, they're energetic, they're enthusiastic, and they're each at least eighty-five.

"Sure; I'll call them." He hesitates. "I'm always nervous about calling, you know? I mean at their age, I hope they're still around to answer the phone."

"They're in great shape, Sam. They'll outlive us all; gefilte fish is the key to eternal youth."

"Okay, I'll call them."

"Thanks, team," I say. "You did great work, and I view all of this as a positive."

"How so?" Laurie asks.

"Well, our operating assumption is that this case is about money. If the money is dirty, that makes it more likely that we are right."

I haven't been to Charlie's Sports Bar in almost two weeks.

In past years, a statement like that would have meant that I was either out of the country or hospitalized. I used to go to Charlie's almost every night to watch sports, eat burgers, and drink beer. Then I got married, and we adopted Ricky, and it seemed like a good time to transition into responsible adulthood.

My two Charlie's buddies have made no such transition. Vince Sanders, the editor of the largest newspaper in North Jersey, and Pete Stanton, the captain of the Homicide Division of the Paterson Police Department, still occupy our regular table almost every night.

They obviously enjoy it, but they also have an economic interest in maintaining their attendance record. All the food and drink they consume goes on my tab; it's pretty hard to walk away from totally free sustenance. And when you throw in thirty-two flat-screen televisions showing sports, it's impossible to resist.

I'm on the way there now and looking forward to it. A couple of hours of eating, drinking, and trading insults will be relaxing and mind cleansing.

Sure enough, Vince and Pete are sitting there when I arrive. The third chair, mine, is still there, perhaps as a silent-yet-sincere tribute to their benefactor. I wonder if they also eat a burnt french fry every night in my honor. Just the thought of it makes my eyes fill with tears . . . and my mouth water.

Vince and Pete both have their eyes glued to a television showing the Mets game, so they don't see me walk over. "Good evening, gentlemen," I say, no doubt one of the few times in their lives they have been referred to that way.

"Well, look who's here," Vince says.

"To what do we owe this honor?" Pete says.

"I thought I would come down and watch my money getting spent. Which, by the way, can stop on a moment's notice if you guys don't start getting more pleasant."

"He's got a point, Vince," Pete says. I don't think Pete even brings his wallet to Charlie's anymore.

Vince shakes his head, surprising me. Vince is the cheapest person I know; the last beer he paid for was brewed during the Bush administration, and I'm not talking about George W. "No, he doesn't. He does not have a point. He screwed me."

"I screwed you? How?"

"You're representing Wasserman."

"So?"

"So he killed my Pulitzer. I already had the acceptance speech written for the ceremony in Sweden, or Norway, or Finland . . . I can never tell the difference between those countries. But the women are unbelievable."

"It's Norway, but that's the Nobel Prize, not the Pulitzer. And trust me, the women there would want as little to do with you as the women here do."

"I would have won the Nobel too. I hope you're happy. You're representing the bastard that killed my dream."

The waiter comes over with my beer; the waiters know what I always have and don't bother waiting for me to order it. A burger and the burnt fries will follow shortly. The way this night is starting, I'm going to need a series of beers and a cab home.

"Vince, I'm going to ask you one more time how Tony Wasserman ruined your shot at journalistic glory. Either answer now or shut up and let me watch the game."

"You know Jerry Bridges?"

"The name sounds familiar; I feel like I've seen it lately."

"You've been reading my paper. Jerry is my best reporter."

"Wait a minute. We're talking about Gerald Bridges?"

"Gerald? It's Jerry. You getting formal now?"

I saw the name Gerald Bridges on the list of people who Rachel knew, the one given to me by Lorraine Baumann. This is getting interesting. "What about him?"

"Rachel Morehouse called me about a month ago. She asked me to come see her. She said she had heard nothing but good things about me as a journalist."

Pete snorts his derision at the statement, but doesn't say anything.

"So you went to see her?"

"Of course; she was a billionaire. Who says no to billionaires?"

"Other billionaires?" I ask.

"Yeah, well, I ain't one of them. I went to see her at her house in Upper Saddle River. You wouldn't believe this house."

"I probably would, but go on."

"She told me she was going to give me an exclusive on a story, that it would be a huge one . . . that once we broke it, the national news would be all over it." Vince shakes his head.

"Did she tell you what it was?"

"No. She wasn't ready. She said that going too early would ruin everything."

"So where does Gerald Bridges come in?"

"She wanted my top reporter assigned to it, so I put Jerry on it. I told him to keep me posted every step of the way."

"And did he?"

"Yeah, for all the good it did me. She gave Jerry almost nothing;

kept telling him the time was getting closer. He kept going to see her, but got the same answer."

"I need to speak to Bridges," I say.

"Is that why you showed up tonight? To pump me and my staff for information?"

"No, I came down to cancel my tab."

Vince's tone changes immediately. "Hey, come on, we're all friends here. Why are we talking about tabs? You know I'd be happy to have you meet Jerry. I'll even drive you to his place if you need a ride."

"You're a true friend, Vince. But I have a question."

"Anything at all, buddy."

"Since I wasn't involved in the case until after Rachel had died, how could I have screwed up your story?"

"You thought I was serious about that? I was joking. Come on, have another beer. It's on you." He takes out his phone. "And wait until you see these pictures of Duchess."

Pete groans when he hears this. Vince recently, and involuntarily, got a golden retriever puppy named Duchess. In a matter of days he went from having nothing to do with dogs to worshipping this one.

"That's okay, Vince," I say. "I've seen more pictures of her than I have of Ricky."

"She's not just cute. She's also smart as hell. I've never seen anything like it."

Pete says, "If she was so smart, she'd run away from home."

"You don't get it, Pete. Andy and I are dog people; we understand."

Pete turns to me. "How do you feel about being in the same group as Vince?"

"I'm not thrilled about it."

can't do that, Andy. I'd be throwing my life away for something that I haven't done."

I've just presented Kathryn Strickland's plea deal offer to Tony Wasserman, and his reaction is what I expected.

"I understand, and as I said, my bringing it to you in no way means I think you should accept it, or that it's a reasonable offer. It's just my obligation to give you the option. I personally think it's a terrible deal."

"Does this bad an offer mean they think they have a strong case?"

"There are two reasons, and one is, yes, they think they have a strong case, and that's because they do. But all prosecution cases are strong until they're challenged. That's the process."

"So we can win?"

"I have no idea. We've just started investigating." I am always truthful with my clients, especially when it comes to their prospects. They deserve it. And Tony seems to be handling his incarceration surprisingly well; first-timers usually have a look of desperation on their face by now.

"You said there were two reasons."

"Right. The other is that it's such a visible case and has and will continue to attract a lot of media attention. They would look bad if they let you off relatively easily."

"I understand. Rachel was rich and people follow the money."

"Correct. Speaking of money, did Rachel talk to you about the business at all?"

He thinks for a moment. "Indirectly. She said she had a lot to do, but not a lot of time to do it."

"Was she referring to the fact that she was sick and might die?"

"That's how I took it. But I don't know it for a fact."

"Did she seem worried? Anxious? Afraid?"

"No, at least she didn't show that to me. I would say she seemed driven. It surprised me, because in that respect she seemed like my father. I never understood them as a match; they came across as such different people. But then I saw this other side of her; she appeared almost obsessed."

"But she didn't say what that was about?"

"No. Maybe it was a way to avoid thinking about her illness. But I'm a chemist, not a psychologist."

I leave after Tony extracts a promise that I will keep him updated on developments, though I caution him that this is a long process.

I head down to my office, not because I'm planning to do any work there; my house is basically our home base. But Sam Willis has an office right down the hall, and I've said he could use mine because his is too small to host the Bubeleh Brigade.

The brigade consists of Hilda and Eli Mandlebaum and Leon Goldberg. Morris Fishman used to be part of the team as well, but he opted for the sunny climate of South Florida. The last we heard he was the shuffleboard champion of Sunrise Lakes, Phase 3. That is quite an accomplishment because Phase 3 is considered a hotbed of shuffleboard talent.

Hilda, in addition to being a whiz on a computer, is probably the best baker in America. I would match her rugelach up against that of anyone else on the planet. And she always makes some for me; if I wasn't married to Laurie and was in the market for an eighty-seven-year-old Jewish great-grandmother, Hilda would be my hands-down choice.

So as soon as I walk in and say hello to everyone, I start sniffing around for the rugelach. Hilda figures out what I'm looking for and says, "There was no time for me to make any, Andy. Sam said this was urgent."

"Sam," I say, "we need to have a conversation about priorities." I turn to the group. "So how is it going, team? Can I get you anything at all? Anything you need? Like maybe an oven and some baking sheets?"

Hilda promises to make a batch tonight, so I ask about progress on the case.

"We're getting there, Andy," Sam says. "But we're talking about thirty-one companies, and there's four of us. You can do the math. And it makes it a bit harder that we don't know what we're looking for."

He's obviously got a point, so I don't push it. Instead I leave, so they can get back to work. I stop downstairs and buy some ripe peaches and watermelon from Sofia Hernandez at her fruit stand below my office.

It's not rugelach, but it's really good stuff.

When I get home I take Tara, Sebastian, and Hunter for a long walk.

One of the negatives of taking on a case is that I don't get to spend enough time with either the dogs or humans that live in our home with me, so I try to make up for it whenever I can.

With Ricky heading for overnight camp in a few days, Laurie and I told him he could pick the restaurant we go to for dinner tonight. He chose Jade Fortune in Paramus. Ricky loves Chinese food, and so do I, but it leaves me dreading the "chopstick moment."

Laurie and Ricky handle chopsticks like they grew up in Beijing, but I simply cannot. If I was forced to use them, I would starve. Since the whole point of going out to eat is not to starve, I always ask for a fork. It is inevitably a humiliating moment, made worse by the smirks and winks that Laurie and Ricky always share with each other.

It's not just embarrassing, it's nonsensical. Even for the most adept chopstickians, it has to be more difficult than using a fork. Experts think that China will lead the world in the coming century? No chance. Just look at a pair of chopsticks and a fork, and you tell me who is more advanced.

I tried arguing the point with Laurie once and got nowhere. I asked why she uses them, and she said that it's a Chinese restaurant, so that's the custom. "Besides," she said, "it's fun and it's easy."

"Fun and easy?" I repeated. "Then why don't you use them elsewhere? Why not at home? Why limit the fun and ease to Chinese restaurants? Why not use them to eat pizza? Or a BLT?"

"Andy, you just keep using a fork, and that way everyone is happy."

"You and Ricky silently mock me."

"Of course we mock you. That's part of the fun."

Tonight the chopstick moment is not as bad as usual because we come here a lot, so the waiter remembered to bring me a fork without me asking. "Oh, a fork?" I say as if surprised. "Well, since it's here, I might as well use it." I can still see Laurie and Ricky winking and smirking, but I'm getting used to it.

The other thing about this restaurant that bugs me is that it serves family-style. I don't do well at this at all; family style is in great conflict with Andy Carpenter style. I always avoid taking my share, holding back because I want Laurie and Ricky to have enough of what they want. So when the dishes start to get low, I stop taking any for fear of leaving them hungry.

Laurie and Ricky have no such concerns, and they suck up everything on the plates. By the time they're finished using their chopsticks on the dishes, I have nothing to stick my fork into. I invariably leave the place hungry.

Even with all of that, the meal is pleasant. We spend the entire time laughing, though for Laurie and me it's bittersweet. Ricky will be leaving soon for the eight-week session at camp, and like every summer, we will miss the hell out of him.

We never talk about a case in front of Ricky. I don't want him telling some future therapist that his parents talked about murder all the time. Another reason for not talking about it tonight is that we haven't gotten anywhere so far. Lack of progress is a real conversation killer.

Ricky loves fortune cookies, so they bring some over. I'm hoping mine says, *You will get an acquittal for Tony Wasserman and you'll be hailed as a genius far and wide.*

But it doesn't.

Instead it says, *The gods that were smiling when you were born are laughing at you now.*

James Wolford is the second Wolford I have gotten to interview on this case. I talked to his wife, Susan, earlier.

We're at the office of Wasserman Equities in Montclair, right off Route 46. They have their own building, but it's fairly small, not the kind of place you would think that billionaires work. But since the company only has eighteen employees, it doesn't feel cramped.

I wonder if they are going to change the name of the company, since all of the Wassermans who were involved are dead. On the other hand, the Wasserman estate still technically owns the place.

Wolford is one of two people that have been referred to as "right-hand men" to Stanley Wasserman when he was alive. The other is Carl Simmons. I suppose the corporate competitive culture prevented either man from wanting to be referred to as a "left-hand man," which resulted in an overload on Stanley's right side.

They've been running the place since Stanley died, so they would have been reporting to Rachel when she arrived on the scene. I have no idea what she thought of them; I never had the chance or the reason to ask her.

I tell the receptionist that I have an appointment with James Wolford, and in less than a minute the word comes back that he's ready to see me. Obviously Wolford never worked at the jail, where he would have learned to keep lawyers waiting.

He's sitting behind his desk when I arrive and looks up as if surprised I've arrived so soon; I'm not sure where he thinks the receptionist was bringing me from. But he smiles and reaches out to shake my hand.

"Thanks for seeing me."

"Robbie Divine can be pretty persuasive. And then my wife said you were pleasant enough."

"Yes, we sat in the sitting room, which seemed appropriate."

He doesn't react to the sitting-room line; it's possible I need new material. "So what can I do for you? I certainly have no information that can help your client; I've never even met him."

"I understand. At this point I'm just trying to acclimate my-self to the environment of the case."

"Which means what?"

"Well, someone in Rachel Morehouse's life killed her. So the first thing I have to do is learn about her life. Friends, business associates, interests . . ."

"Well, happy to tell you what I know. I was both a friend and a business associate."

"Good. Let's start with your business. You buy companies, run them for a while, and then often sell them?"

"Rather than tell you how your description is inaccurate and incomplete, let me tell you what we do. We find opportunities and then invest in them. But to maximize our return on those investments, we usually want to control them. So if we think we can improve management, we do so. If we are satisfied that current management is top-of-the-line, we keep them in place.

"Sometimes we get those businesses to the point where we can sell them and get an excellent return; sometimes it's in our interest to keep them. We are flexible in that way."

None of this is news to me, but I let him go through it. "What kind of businesses do you buy?"

"The kind that make money."

"Are you continuing to execute Stanley Wasserman's philosophy?"

Wolford nods. "We are, allowing for changing times. Stanley was brilliant."

"And Rachel?"

"Wonderful woman. Whoever killed her deserves the worst the system can provide."

"I understand she was involving herself in the business?"

He nods. "As was her right. But she was very respectful and was interested in learning. She was a quick study, possibly because she spent so much time with Stanley."

"You knew she was ill?"

He nods again. "We all did. But she never let it get her down."

"If she was so ill, and unlikely to survive, why do you think she wanted to learn the business? I mean, she must have known she wouldn't be around to run it."

"It's an excellent question, and one I can't answer. Maybe she wasn't so pessimistic about her survival chances. She was a very determined woman. Or maybe she just had an insatiable desire to learn and experience new things; many people are like that. In any event, she was an asset and a pleasure to have around."

"Were you and Stanley and Rachel and Susan personal friends? I mean outside the office. Did you double-date much?"

Wolford smiles. "I haven't heard that expression in a while. I would say we were friends; certainly we spent a lot of time together at industry functions, charity dinners, that kind of thing. But keep in mind that Stanley was technically my boss; I assume you're familiar with that dynamic?"

"Nope."

"You've never had a boss?" he asks, skeptical.

"Just my wife and son, and they're not that strict. They even let me use a fork at Jade Fortune last night."

"I'm happy for you."

"You're probably a chopsticks guy."

"We seem to be getting rather far afield here, and I'm quite busy."

I nod. "Just wrapping up. So Carl Simmons is your equal here? You're both sitting at the top of the totem pole?"

"We're co-CEOs."

"What happens if you don't agree on something?"

"We talk it out and come to a position we can both live with. Stanley taught us both, so our philosophies are basically similar."

"Any chance Rachel Morehouse was going to get rid of you?"

Wolford's voice turns noticeably colder. "There was certainly no indication of that."

"What about Carl?"

"Same answer."

"Any idea who would have profited from killing Rachel Morehouse?"

"The police seem to think the answer is your client."

"Yeah. I hate when that happens."

Andy, I just want to update you on where things stand."

It's Bernie Hudson, and I hope he's talking about the privilege issue he discussed with me and not the $2 million from Rachel's will. When I get the money, I'm going to have to figure out what to do with it, and I don't have the time right now.

"Okay, Bernie. I'm sitting on my recliner in listening position."

"I went to Judge Lofton like you said; he couldn't have been nicer about it. He immediately waived the privilege and directed me to share the information with the police. He said that you would then get it as part of discovery."

"Good."

"But I thought I'd share it with you as well. Just in case they don't provide it, or it takes them a while to do so."

"Great. I appreciate it." I love situations like this, where I know something and wait for the prosecution to provide it. That way if they don't for any reason, I have a ready-made complaint for appeal, or maybe sanctions against them by the judge.

It doesn't usually happen, and in this situation it's even less likely that the information would be withheld because the prosecution would be aware that the judge already knows about it. But I live in hope.

"So I don't know which way it cuts," Bernie says. "But Rachel had set up an appointment with me to amend her will. I don't know how, but I do know it involved your client, at least in part."

"She told you that?"

"She did. It was a brief conversation, and I don't know if she was going to leave him more or cut him out entirely. She said she had some things to do first."

"Did she say what those things were?"

"No. We were scheduled to meet three days after she died."

I pump him with a few more questions, but there is nothing more to be learned. He just doesn't know anything else.

There's nothing earthshaking about this news, and like everything else about the situation with Rachel's will, it can fit neatly into a prosecution theory.

They will imply that Rachel was cutting Tony out entirely, and we will argue the reverse, that she was giving him a larger piece.

If Tony is to be believed, and I do believe him, nothing happened to cause her to reverse Stanley's wish to leave his son the $300,000. I'm sure Stanley saw such a paltry sum as a slap in the face to Tony.

Most people would view it differently; my mother used to say about any sum of money that you could walk all the way to California, looking down, and not find that much in the street. The jury will likely see it as a significant sum, one Tony might kill to avoid losing.

Or, they could think that Tony would believe it was billions less than he was hoping for, and he killed out of anger and bitterness.

"It's time to go," Laurie says, interrupting my thoughts.

She's standing in the doorway with Ricky. He is wearing his

camp T-shirt, an unnecessary reminder that he leaves for camp today. All we do is take him to the camp bus stop in Ridgewood, but we do it as a family event.

Tara, Sebastian, and Hunter come along as well, although we could use a crane to get Sebastian up and into the car. He is not inclined to help; he prefers to stand there and get hoisted. I am unfortunately the designated hoister.

It's Ricky's third year at camp, and I'm getting better at dealing with it, though only marginally. I still have a lump in my throat the size of New Zealand.

Ricky always has a great time at camp and is anxious to go. I'm happy about this but also a bit annoyed at his glee at leaving home. Laurie says to get over it, so I am working at getting over it.

When we get to the bus stop, a mass of parents are milling around, but most of the kids are on the waiting bus, which isn't scheduled to leave for a half hour. Ricky looks at the bus, then looks at us, and clearly makes the decision that the bus is the place to be.

He hugs us good-bye and runs off to his friends. Only two members of our family are emotional, me and Laurie, though Tara's expression is solemn, as she no doubt understands the significance of the moment.

We wait for the bus to pull away, as do all the other parents. Ricky waves to us from the window, but he's throwing us a bone and doesn't even watch to see if we wave back. Which, of course, we do.

Laurie's face is wet, the source of the moisture being her eyes. I'm busy trying to deal with the aforementioned throat lump.

On the way home, with no twelve-year-old impressionable humans in the car, we are free to talk about the case. It only adds to the day's depression.

"My problem is I don't yet have a theory of the case. I have the vague feeling that the murder was tied into her entry into the business, but I've got nothing factual to point to. I can't even convince myself."

"Nothing to take to the jury," Laurie says, more a statement than a question.

"No. Tony had the opportunity, the know-how, and, in the eyes of the prosecution, a motive. He also had the trace evidence in the car and his room, which is very incriminating."

She nods. "So we do what we always do. Just keep plugging along until we figure it out."

"Right. And the upside is if we have to go somewhere to solve the case, we don't have to get a babysitter."

I drop Laurie off at home and head down to the jail to see my client. It's not something I look forward to because Tony will inevitably hope I am bringing good news, and I'm not.

Tony is more upbeat than almost every other client I have had in this situation. He tries to cheer me up, the reverse of what should be happening.

"You'll get there, Andy."

I always try to be realistic and not raise false hope. "Sometimes we do, and sometimes we don't. You need to understand that."

He smiles. "I choose not to."

As soon as the phone rings to wake me, even before I answer it, I look toward the digital clock on the night table.

It's the way I judge these kind of calls; the deeper into the night that they take place, the more chance that it's an emergency or bad news. I could just answer it and find out, but first I look at the clock to be prepared.

The time is 6:35, and then I realize that it's not dark out anymore. This drastically reduces the chance for disaster, so I pick up the phone with some confidence.

"Hello?"

"Hey, Andy, it's Sam."

"Hey, Sam, it's early."

"I know, but I think we found something interesting. The whole team is here, and—"

"They're all in your office at six thirty in the morning?"

"Actually, it's your office, but, yes, they are. Andy, these people get up at four o'clock in the morning."

"They do?"

"Yup. It turns out there's a whole subculture out there of elderly Jewish night people who are awake when we're asleep. And you know what? They're converting me; it's amazing what can be accomplished with the extra time."

"I'm a non-elderly day person, Sam; please keep that in mind. What did you come up with?"

"Can I come over and show you?"

"Sam, why don't you just tell me and . . . wait a minute. Did Hilda bake any rugelach?"

"She did. It's fantastic. You want some?"

"Sam, you can go your whole life without asking a dumber question than that. Bring it over here and hurry up; the day is wasting away."

I get up quickly and go find Laurie. I do that by following the sound of heavy breathing; as she does every morning, Laurie is pedaling furiously to nowhere on her exercise bike.

This time her video screen shows her riding in the rolling hills of Tuscany. She passes some guy along the route; he doesn't take a second look at her, which proves the whole thing is fake.

I think and hope that she's not fooled, that she realizes she's actually still on the cement streets of Paterson, New Jersey. But I'm not about to ask.

I tell her that Sam is coming over with some information, and she nods and starts pedaling even faster. I guess she wants to get to Florence or wherever she's going before he arrives.

I jump in the shower and then quickly get dressed. I'm downstairs and hungry when Sam rings the bell. I let him in, reaching my hand out. He thinks I'm going to shake hands, but I'm actually grabbing the package he is holding.

"Let's talk in the kitchen," I say.

We head in there with me opening the bag along the way. By the time Laurie arrives moments later I am inhaling Hilda's creations. Laurie just looks at me, and then the rugelach, and surprises me by saying, "Give me one of those."

She grabs one and says, "What have you got, Sam?"

"I'm not sure, but it struck us as interesting. Leon is really the one who made the connection—"

"Land the plane, Sam." That is my way of encouraging him to move things along. Sam gives lengthy preambles to his reports; they are often longer than the reports themselves. I think he relishes the spotlight, even when it's in our kitchen at seven o'clock in the morning.

"A guy named Matt Reisinger was the CEO of a company called Global Aviation in Cincinnati when Wasserman Equities bought his company about three and a half years ago. They kept him in place but brought in a few key employees right under him, which is sort of a pattern of theirs.

"A little more than three years ago, he went for a hike in the mountains of North Carolina, about an hour from Asheville. According to media reports, he would do that at least a couple of times a year; it was the way he refreshed himself, by camping and living in the wilderness."

Personally I don't understand the whole "living in the wilderness" thing. I thought things like houses and plumbing and restaurants were invented strictly for the purpose of avoiding that approach.

At this moment, one of the modern conveniences that I am particularly grateful for is ovens. If Hilda Mandlebaum lived in the wilderness without an oven, I'd be eating berries and tree bark right now. But I don't want to mention that because I don't want to slow Sam down.

Instead Laurie asks, "So what happened to him?"

"He fell over the edge of a cliff to his death. Two hundred feet. The case was investigated by the North Carolina State Police and the death was ruled as accidental."

"But you have reason to believe it was not accidental?" I ask.

"I have no idea one way or the other. But his wife was very vocal about it, saying that he was an experienced hiker and this could not have happened to him. She thought the police closed the case way too quickly."

"That's not uncommon, Sam," Laurie says. "People often don't want to accept that any little thing, maybe a misstep in this case, can totally alter their world."

Sam nods. "I agree. And if that was all that was going on, I wouldn't be sitting here watching Andy disgustingly gorge himself on rugelach. But there's more."

"More how?" I mumble the words since my mouth is full, confirming Sam's assessment of my actions.

He looks at us like the cat who ate the canary. "At three of Wasserman's other companies, a top executive died within six months of their taking over. In one of those cases, the executive had just been replaced, in the other two they were still in their position. In all these situations, executives had been brought in by Wasserman and put in positions directly under them."

"Died how?"

"One ran Wasserman's trucking company; he had a sudden heart attack. Another was a hit-and-run victim; she ran Wasserman's headhunting company. The third, who was the CEO of Wasserman's pharmaceutical company, apparently died of some kind of allergic reaction. I don't have any more details than that."

"And in the heart attack and allergy cases, no foul play was alleged?"

"Doesn't seem to have been, though I don't yet have access to the police records."

I note Sam's use of the word *yet*. I was once uncomfortable using him to illegally penetrate all these places, but I've long ago gotten over it.

"Have you looked at all thirty-one companies yet?" Laurie asks.

He shakes his head. "No, at this point maybe twenty-three. We ran into a delay because my team won't hack into websites on the Sabbath."

I nod. "'Thou shall not hacketh . . .' I think it's the second or third commandment."

There are many occupations with the kind of connection links that would surprise even Kevin Bacon.

Lawyering is a perfect example. If someone asked me to recommend an attorney, say, in Iowa, I could probably do so even though I don't presently know anyone that lives there.

Maybe a law school buddy mentioned a friend from there, or a local lawyer met someone at one of the legal conventions I never attend. The point is, if I put out the word, I could find someone in a short time.

I imagine the same is true of doctors and accountants and tech guys, and whatever. But nobody has a connective chain like cops.

When I told Laurie and Corey Douglas that I wanted to talk to a cop in the Asheville, North Carolina, area about Matt Reisinger, they sprang into action. Three hours later I had an appointment to meet with Lieutenant Don Emerson of the North Carolina State Police.

Depending on what I hear from Emerson, I might go on to Cincinnati, where Reisinger lived and worked. But I'll only do it if I think there is anything here worth pursuing.

Certainly the stuff Sam and his team came up with is interesting, and at the least extremely coincidental. I'm not a big believer in coincidences, which is why I've made this trip.

I flew down last night and stayed at an airport hotel in Charlotte. I like airport hotels, the main reason being they are at airports. When I fly to some place, I generally don't like to get lost. Airport hotels are easy to find.

They also have a readily available continental breakfast, served buffet-style. I can get coffee and fruit and whatever quickly and without having to smile at a waiter or waitress, or call for a check, or use a cloth napkin.

I grab breakfast and head for the state police office in Charlotte to meet with Lieutenant Emerson. He's not there at nine o'clock, which was when the appointment was scheduled for, and he doesn't show up until nine forty-five. No apology is forthcoming.

We go back to his office. I have no idea of the connection chain that got me in to see him, and it doesn't matter. He seems like a no-nonsense guy, and he starts with "You wanted to talk about Reisinger?"

"Right."

"Why?"

"I have a case that may be indirectly related to his. Probably not, but it seemed worth pursuing."

"What did you want to know?"

"If the death was accidental."

"That's the official word."

"And you think that's right?"

He pauses for a moment, as if trying to decide how he should answer. "Bottom line? No, I don't buy it. Guy was an experienced hiker, and his stuff was neatly packed and ready to go. So before he leaves, he walks over to the other side and slips? It's possible, but I don't think so."

"Then what happened?"

"I think he was pushed or tossed. But we could never find any evidence of it, so we had no choice but to call it accidental."

"Could he have killed himself?"

"And drive all the way here to do it? They have buildings and probably bridges in Cincinnati he could jump off that would do the trick. I mean, you never know what is going on in someone's mind, but that would be pretty strange. And a rich guy like that . . . just doesn't make sense to me."

"Rich people can have problems and kill themselves. Richard Cory did."

"You believe everything Simon and Garfunkel tell you?" he asks.

"Actually, I do, although I have my doubts that there are fifty ways to leave a lover. No one saw anyone on the trail?"

"No. Nothing. If someone killed him, he was either very good or very lucky."

"Did you deal with anyone in Cincinnati? Maybe to find out if he had enemies?"

Emerson frowns. "No . . . is that what big-city cops would do?" He gets up and goes to his file cabinet. He takes out a folder, skims through it. "Lieutenant Anthony, Cincinnati PD. Good guy. I told him if he dug up anything that I could use on this end to let me know."

"You never heard back from him?"

"No."

"But you have doubts."

He nods. "Doubts aren't evidence. You're a lawyer, right? You know that better than anyone."

"I'm afraid I do."

"You come up with anything, I want to hear about it."

"You can count on that. Thanks for your time."

"You going to Cincinnati?"

I nod. "I hear it's beautiful this time of year."

t doesn't make sense to go home and then go to Cincinnati, so I am flying there on a direct flight from Charlotte.

One of the fantastic things about my job is all the incredibly exotic places I get to visit.

Corey and Laurie have once again worked their magic, and I have a meeting tomorrow with Lieutenant Anthony, the guy that Emerson said he talked to about the case. Even better, the Mets are in town so I am going to the game tonight.

The Reds play in what's called the Great American Ball Park. That might be an exaggeration, but it's a nice place. Starting with Camden Yards in Baltimore, teams have learned how to build stadiums that are beautiful and customer friendly.

I once wanted to be able to say that I saw a game at every major-league park. That's another dream that went by the wayside, partially because they keep knocking them down and building new ones. At this point I've been to seven current parks.

The stadium is on Joe Nuxhall Way. Nuxhall was and is the youngest player ever to play in a major-league game, having pitched at the age of fifteen. Everybody seems to think that's a big deal. My greatest accomplishment at fifteen was dating Susan Rossiter, something I am sure Nuxhall was never able to do.

The announced crowd of twenty-four thousand seems about

six thousand too generous, and I'm pretty sure that I'm the only Mets fan in the place. I'm also the only disappointed fan in the place, because the Mets lose 7–2, after leading 2–0 in the sixth.

I head back to my airport hotel after room service is closed, so I'm reduced to getting pretzels and soda from the vending machine. My life is glamorous.

My plan today is to see Lieutenant Anthony and then visit with Reisinger's wife. Laurie had called her to set it up and related that she seemed eager to talk. That fits neatly with what Sam said about media reports that she did not believe her husband's death was accidental.

The state police office buildings in Cincinnati look remarkably similar to those in Charlotte, and none of them will appear in *Architectural Digest*. The same could be said of the interiors, and Anthony has an office that could double for Emerson's.

Both cops are similarly direct and to the point. "So Emerson called me this morning; he said you think Matt Reisinger was murdered," Anthony says.

"I actually have no opinion on the matter at all, but I am interested in what you think."

"I think it's bullshit. The guy was walking along a ledge, which is nuts to begin with, and he fell. Maybe he was drinking, or maybe the sun was in his eyes."

"He was an experienced hiker and had been on that trail at least a dozen times." I'm actually making the number up, but it sounds good. "And it was first thing in the morning, so drinking anything other than coffee is unlikely."

"So? So he got overconfident and made a stupid mistake. It happens. I tripped walking down the steps of my house a couple of years ago and broke my ankle. Nobody pushed me."

"I understand his wife feels otherwise?"

"And if she had any evidence, she would have given it to us. But there was nothing."

"Did you investigate his situation within his business?"

"We talked to the appropriate people; they're executives, not murderers. And if they were going to kill him, would they follow him to North Carolina? Cincinnati's not a nice enough town to commit a murder in?"

I'm realizing that I made a mistake here; I should have spoken to Reisinger's wife first. That would have made me more knowledgeable about the situation and have given me more things to possibly challenge Anthony with.

Instead I'm sitting here talking to a cop who decided years ago that this was not a murder, and asking him if he thinks it was a murder.

Not a productive approach.

At his core, though, Anthony seems like a good cop, and he asks me to please alert him if I come up with anything worth pursuing. I promise to do that, even though I am not optimistic that will be the case.

I am going to talk to Reisinger's wife and will no doubt hear the same things she must have told Anthony and the media. If no one found that compelling, and I have to assume that's the case, there is little reason that I will feel otherwise.

One thing I am not going to do is hang around to go to another Mets game. Come tonight, I am heading back to the glorious summer playground that is Paterson, New Jersey.

Samantha Reisinger is waiting on her front porch for me when I pull up. It's a beautiful old Southern-style home with a wraparound porch, with the nearest neighbor at least a quarter of a mile away.

It's surrounded by acres of manicured grass, too large to be called a lawn in the way I think about it. The whole place is contained by brown fencing, all of which looks polished, and I'm assuming that the large barn off to the side contains horses.

"Mr. Carpenter, thank you so much for coming." She extends her hand as I reach the porch. It's a strange thing to say, as if she had summoned me, rather than my instigating the meeting.

"Thanks for seeing me on such short notice." I follow her into the house.

The inside also maintains the Southern style, and ceiling fans slowly turn above us. It's relatively cool out today, but if these fans are expected to do the job on hot summer days, they are going to disappoint.

We go into the den and she offers me coffee or tea to go with the clearly homemade cookies that are already sitting there. It's not Hilda's rugelach, but it looks a hell of a lot better than the hotel muffins I sucked down this morning.

Once we're settled and I've complimented her on the house,

Samantha, as she insists I call her, says, "Your wife, Laurie, said you wanted to talk to me about Matt's murder."

I'm glad that she referred to my "wife Laurie"; otherwise I might have thought Samantha was talking about my wife Clara or my wife Lucinda. But in any event, I'm quite certain that's not how Laurie would have characterized my reason for being here. So I correct Samantha by saying, "I really haven't made any judgments about it; it seems to fit a pattern that may be a coincidence, but it may not."

This certainly piques her interest. "So other people have been killed as well? These killers must be stopped."

"I'm not ready to say that yet. But I would like to hear your view. I spoke to Lieutenant Anthony, and he believes it was a tragic accident."

"Was he there?"

"No."

"Did he know Matt?"

"I have no idea."

"Well, I knew my husband, and he was the most careful man I have ever been around. Do you know he taught courses at the Y on outdoor safety? There is simply no way he could have carelessly slipped. I have been hiking with him many times, and I am telling you there is no way."

"Did he know people in North Carolina? People that would have wanted to cause him harm?"

She shakes her head. "This had nothing to do with North Carolina or any people there. The killers are here, in Cincinnati."

"Who are they?"

"The people at Matt's company. He built that place from scratch, and the biggest mistake he ever made was selling it. It cost him his life."

"What makes you say that?"

"They brought people in under him, and Matt saw what they were doing. They are criminals and he knew it. He was going to bring them down."

"What were they doing?"

She almost moans in frustration. "I don't know; he didn't tell me. He always tried to protect me. But he was going to deal with it when he got back. Those trips gave him strength in difficult times, and this was going to be very difficult."

"But he never said what it was?"

"No. There's not a day that goes by that I don't wish he did. I could have carried on the fight; I could have exposed them. There's just one thing. . . ."

"What's that?"

"The day he left, he got a phone call from a woman who ran a headhunter kind of company, the kind that places people in jobs? I answered the phone, but when I put him on, he went in his office and closed the door. That was unlike him. Maybe he was looking for another job, but I don't think so; that's the kind of thing he would have told me."

This is interesting to me because Sam said that the woman CEO who ran Wasserman's headhunting company was a hit-and-run victim. "Did you get her name?"

"I just don't remember it."

"Is there anyone at your husband's company, either then or now, that might have more information? Someone I could talk to?"

She is silent for a while. "There might be . . . if they haven't killed him also."

"Who is this?"

"Stephen Gilley. He worked for Matt. After Matt died, he quit his job, moved out of his apartment, and left town. He was a single guy, and as far as I know, no one knew where he went."

"Did you talk about him with the police?"

She nods. "Yes. They weren't interested. They said he wasn't a missing person, that he left voluntarily and as an adult could do so. I tried to find him, but I couldn't."

"Why do you think he left?"

"He was afraid; there's no other explanation. There can't be."

"Why do you think he was afraid?"

"Because he had to know, or at least suspect, that Matt was murdered. He was Matt's right-hand man; whatever Matt knew, he knew."

"What can you tell me about him that could help me find him?"

"Not much; for all I know they could have found and killed him also. I just know his name and that he was originally from a small town in Maine called Wilton. I actually went there, but he had no family there anymore, and since he had been gone for so long, no one that I could find knew him."

That she went to Maine obviously shows how strongly she feels about this. But there are easier ways to track people down, like using Sam Willis. "How old is Gilley?"

She thinks for a moment. "Let's see, forty-three or forty-four."

"And you haven't been in touch with him since he left?"

She hesitates; which is the same as holding up a sign saying I'M ABOUT TO LIE. "No."

"So Gilley never contacted you?"

Another hesitation. "No." She's such a bad liar that I wouldn't be surprised if she and Gilley played bridge together every Thursday night.

I press the issue a bit, but she won't back off, so I leave. I do so reluctantly because there is still one cookie left on the plate. Laurie would be proud.

Samantha asks me to please tell her if I learn anything, and I promise that I will. It's the same promise I made to Lieutenants

Emerson and Anthony. Everybody seems to be counting on me to make progress; all signs are that they will be sorely disappointed.

My guess, and it's only a guess, is that she has, or at least had, been in contact with Gilley. She may have promised not to reveal his location, but I think she'd be pleased if we found him without her having to break that promise.

I head for the airport. There is a flight in two hours and I am going to be on it. On the way I call Sam and tell him to put the team on the task of finding Stephen Gilley. Sam promises to do so and tells me they found another case at one of Wasserman's companies that might fit into the pattern.

I don't ask him to give me the details because I'm reaching the airport. I'll hear about it when I get home.

I am anxious to get home.

They went by the names Chris Marrero and Roy Callison.

Those were not their real names; by now they almost forgot what their real names were. After seven years here, they felt like they were Americans, even if their loyalties were elsewhere.

Marrero and Callison had seen each other just five times in those seven years, the same number of times they had seen the man known to them as Stal. Marrero lived in Detroit and Houston, while Callison lived in Atlanta and Chicago; they were placed in large cities to help preserve their anonymity.

Both claimed they were truck drivers, a lie that was bolstered by their each living in two cities. They would live in each place for two weeks at a time, consistent with the life of a truck driver who would go on a two-week assignment, then be off for two weeks.

Even though they were careful to avoid close relationships, neighbors could be curious, so the precautions that they took made their lifestyle seem credible.

Each time they met with Stal, it was in Philadelphia. The sessions could conceivably have been done by telephone, but Stal felt it was more effective to meet in person. That way he could more easily confirm that they were conducting themselves professionally, and taking steps to maintain their privacy.

There was also the intimidation. As dangerous and violent as Marrero and Callison could be, Stal was on another level. Seeing him in person was a probably unnecessary reminder of that; Stal carried with him a menace and danger that was inescapable.

Their meetings generally did not last more than a few minutes. Stal was not a person to make small talk or discuss anything other than the matter at hand. This time was no exception.

He began with a question: "Did either of you have anything to do with the murder of Wasserman's wife?"

"No," they both said in unison.

"Do you know who did?"

Two more noes.

"It has caused us a problem," Stal said. "It has prompted investigations into areas we do not want investigated."

"What do you want us to do?"

"For the moment, nothing. Just wait for my directive, which may or may not be forthcoming. But in the meantime, read and commit this to memory." Stal handed them each thin folders. "There is a lawyer named Carpenter who has been prying into areas he should not. You will read about him in here. Once you have done so, destroy the papers."

"So he may have to be dealt with?" What Marrero did not ask was which of them might be called on to do the job. They each had their own strengths, and Stal would make that decision based on the circumstances as they arose.

Marrero and Callison had never been called upon to work together. It had never been necessary; one of them had always been more than sufficient to get the job done.

Stal nodded. "He may have to be dealt with."

Gerald Bridges appears to be the exact opposite of his boss, Vince Sanders.

He wears perfectly tailored clothes, including a vest and a bow tie. To say that Vince dresses like a slob is to slander slobs everywhere. Gerald's shirt bears the Brooks Brothers logo; Vince's generally display the Gulden's mustard stain.

Gerald has a pleasant way about him, smiling and affable. Vince's go-to demeanor is snarling and disagreeable. Gerald's manner is respectful; Vince opts for contemptuous.

But Vince is an excellent newspaperman and has been for decades. And Vince says that Gerald is his best reporter. I believe him because if Gerald wasn't any good, Vince would have canned his ass a long time ago.

I meet Gerald at the Starbucks on East Ridgewood Avenue in Ridgewood at 9:00 A.M. He's already there when I arrive and has parked himself and his coffee at an outside table. I say hello and go in, get my black coffee and a piece of banana bread, and come back out.

As soon as I sit down, he gets up to get a coffee refill, explaining that he had arrived early, so he had already finished his first cup. We might be here for hours and never be sitting at the table at the same time.

Fortunately, our schedules work out, and when he comes back, we start talking. We chat for a while about Vince and what an obnoxious character he is, but I can tell that Gerald has a healthy respect for Vince as a journalist.

"So did he tell you why I wanted to talk to you?" I ask.

"About Rachel Morehouse."

"Right. Obviously I'm trying to figure out who killed her, but first I need to know what she was doing in her last days."

He frowns. "Well, she wasn't talking to me. She kept promising to, and throwing out hints, but she never ultimately came through."

"But you kept following up?"

He nods. "Absolutely. There was something there. Rachel did not seem like the type to lead me, and especially herself, on a wild-goose chase. She was a serious person, and I was convinced whatever was going on was potentially a big story."

"So please tell me exactly what she said to you."

"That she was going to hand-deliver a huge story to me. That once we broke it, it would become national news."

"Why did she say she wasn't ready to tell you the details?"

"Because if it got out in any way before she was ready, it would be dangerous."

"Dangerous to the story? Physically dangerous?"

"I think both. She did warn me that once I knew what was happening, especially before publication, I might be in physical danger. She wanted to be sure I understood that and would accept the risks. Obviously I told her that I would do so."

"Did you get the sense it was about the business she inherited?"

He nods. "I definitely did. Not so much because of anything she told me, but her actions led me to believe it. She was spending a lot of time there and seemed to be focused on it. She also asked me if I had a working knowledge of finance, how money was transferred."

"You think she was talking about dirty money?"

He nods. "The thought did cross my mind. But back to your question. I do think it had to be about Wasserman Equities. If there was such a huge story that she was dealing with, I have to think she wouldn't be so involved with the business on a daily basis if it was unrelated."

"Did you ever ask her about the particulars of the business?"

"I did. I said I wanted to know everything, so that when she told me the story, I'd be well versed on her life. One interesting thing is that she referred to the two people who ran the place as 'the people there now.' The implication was that they were not permanent."

"Did she ever mention Tony Wasserman?"

"No, but I met Tony one time when I was visiting her. They seemed to get along quite well."

"Are you still working on the story?"

"Technically yes, but practically no. There are no leads to follow up on for me. I could look into the business, but from the outside I would really have no road map or way to penetrate it. I'm afraid the story died when Rachel did." Then, "Vince is really pissed about it."

"That breaks my heart."

"The only way I can get him to stop complaining is to ask him about his dog. He's nuts about that poor dog. He must drive her crazy."

"I know. She's been rescued once; we may have to do it again."

have no idea what Rachel Morehouse was trying to do in the days before she died.

Nor do I know how she was going to amend her will in her scheduled meeting with Bernie Hudson, other than it was at least partially about Tony.

Nor do I know why she suddenly decided to call me to make sure I would provide for Lion in the event of her death. And my supposition that it was related to her health issues just went at least partially out the window.

Dr. Danielle Vinman, Rachel's oncologist, just shot a hole in that theory. Given direction by Judge Lofton to reveal privileged information about Rachel's medical condition, the doctor sent the information and her opinion to the prosecution, who sent it on to us in discovery.

Rachel's cancer might well have killed her, though that was neither certain nor particularly imminent. Treatment was making substantial progress in decreasing the size of the offending tumor, and there was real hope of long-term remission.

Certainly Rachel was not giving up and expressed optimism to Dr. Vinman the last time they met.

On some level it gives more credibility to Sam's potential conspiracy revelations about events at the Wasserman Equity–controlled companies, and Reisinger's wife's theory about his death. But we are a long distance from forming coherent theories and turning them into defense strategies.

Corey Douglas has just gotten back from Philadelphia, where he was looking into a similar situation to Reisinger's. Philip Callan was the CEO of Winston Pharmaceutical, a midsize drug-manufacturing company that had been purchased by Wasserman.

Eight months after the purchase, he died tragically at the age of forty-one from a reaction triggered by his peanut allergy. As in the case of Reisinger, there was no indication of foul play, and the police did not press any charges or name any suspects.

Corey is back to update us, and Marcus is here as well. Marcus is an excellent investigator, but he has had little involvement in this case so far, for the simple reason that we have not had much to investigate.

But whenever there is even a hint of violent activity, it's prudent to have Marcus involved. Corey and Laurie, as ex-cops, can handle themselves well in physical and potentially dangerous situations. But they are not in Marcus's league in dealing with violent threats; Marcus is the lone member of his own league. He doesn't say anything particularly decipherable to anyone but Laurie, but in his very presence the message he conveys is clear: do not mess with Marcus or anyone on his team.

"Callan lived in a suburb of Philadelphia called Bryn Mawr," Corey says. "His office was in downtown Philly, and they had a small factory near King of Prussia. He was a wealthy guy with a net worth of twenty-eight million. He made most of that in the sale to Wasserman Equity."

"Married?" I ask.

"No, the only family he has in the area is a sister named Janice Roberts. I spoke to her."

"Did you speak to any of the police on the case?" Laurie asks.

"No, because there were no police on the case. There was no case at all. An autopsy was done, and it was determined that Callan died from a severe allergic reaction to a peanut product. It was an allergy he'd had since his youth, with one prior reaction when he was seventeen. At that time he injected himself and survived.

"In this case he was out to eat in a restaurant about a mile from his house. He had walked there; the fastest route was through a small park. He died on the way home, and his body was found in the park."

"Did he eat with anyone?"

"Yes, a friend who lived even closer to the restaurant. The friend did not notice any reason why Callan should have ingested anything to trigger the allergy, and the restaurant vigorously denied negligence. Callan was a regular at the place, and they knew of his allergy and took steps to make sure that they did nothing to harm his health."

"What did the sister have to say?" I ask.

"That the facts as alleged were wrong; that her brother was fanatically careful to not do anything to trigger the allergy, that he was a smart, conservative guy, and he knew that his life depended on it.

"She also said that he would never go anywhere without his EpiPen, and that in fact he carried two of them. She wouldn't go so far as to say he was murdered, but the fact that he didn't have the pens with him simply could not be explained, especially since they were not found at his house."

"Had he been drinking at the restaurant?" Laurie asks.

"No, the autopsy confirmed that he was not impaired."

Laurie asks if Corey spoke to anyone at the company where Callan worked.

"No, the head guy was out of town, or at least that's what

they told me. I left a message for him to call me, but I have no idea if he will."

"Did the sister suspect any wrongdoing at the company?"

Corey shakes his head. "Not really, but she said he rarely if ever discussed business with her. She did say he seemed a bit troubled the last two times they talked, but it was more a vague feeling she had, nothing specific that he had said to her."

"So what's your bottom-line feeling?" I ask.

Corey thinks about it for a moment before answering. "If it wasn't for the coincidences Sam has raised, and if it didn't track so similarly with the Reisinger situation in Cincinnati, I would dismiss this as a tragic accident. But because of those things, I'm not so sure.

"And there's one other thing. I walked the distance from the restaurant to the place where the body was found. It took four minutes; an allergic reaction would generally happen faster than that, and that includes the unlikely assumption he had the exposure to peanuts right as he was leaving the restaurant. That really doesn't make sense to me . . . and I can't imagine he brought a bag of peanuts to eat on the way home.

"So I certainly wouldn't reject out of hand the possibility that this was a murder. It's quite conceivable."

It's a little weird that I'm rooting for it to have been a murder, but as Hyman Roth would say, "This is the business we have chosen."

To cheer myself up I go down to the Tara Foundation and take Lion for a walk. He is always upbeat, and his attitude is infectious. By the time we get back, I'm ready to get back up on the legal horse and ride back into the battle.

We are taking a different approach on this than the local police did.

Mainly that is because we are looking at, or trying to look at, the big picture. Each individual police force would only have been concerned with their own situation. Reisinger was only interesting to the North Carolina and Cincinnati police, Callan to Philadelphia, and so on.

They had no reason to think it tied in any way to the parent company, Wasserman Equities. They saw their local issue as limited to that one death. In Philadelphia, the police didn't get involved at all. I'm sure they were called to the scene when the body was discovered, but they wouldn't naturally think it might be murder, or part of some grand conspiracy.

We have the ability, and certainly the motivation, to look for some overall connection. That is not to say there is one; it could just be a series of coincidences. But if there is a link between the various cases and cities, then it is something to follow through on and dissect in defense of our client.

If we're right, then it's an easy logical jump to tying it all in to the murder of Rachel Morehouse. Proving it to a jury is another thing altogether, but one step at a time.

If we're wrong, and we can't get anywhere with this, then we are in deep trouble in trying to mount a successful defense of

Tony Wasserman. We cannot present any evidence to disprove even a single piece of the prosecution's case, at least not right now.

But these other cases are years old, and no police records are available to help us. We're starting from scratch and from a position far from where we need to be, with not a lot of time to make up the distance.

I call Sam to find out if he and his team have made any progress in locating Stephen Gilley, and I get mixed news. "We might have a lead," he says. "Nothing definitive, but it's possible. If we're right, he's in the Monticello area."

I could ask him the details about why he believes that, but there is no need to. He'll tell me when he has something for sure, and we can follow up then. "Good. Keep on it, Sam. Highest priority."

"Hilda is on it full-time. She's a pit bull. If you owe money, you do not want to find out that Hilda Mandlebaum is your bill collector."

"Excellent. I can't believe I'm actually saying this, but it's more important than rugelach."

"Wow."

I get off the phone. All I can do is hope that Sam and Hilda can locate Gilley, and that he's alive and talkative. Samantha said that she thought he could be dead, murdered by the same people who killed her husband, but I think she was lying. I think she's been in contact with him, and that while she won't betray him, she hopes we find him.

So do I.

What I need to do is start focusing on our defense independent of all of this. Corey and Laurie are going to investigate the other suspicious deaths in the two other companies, and I certainly hope that amounts to something. But if it doesn't, I have to be ready.

None of this means the dogs don't have to be walked, so I take the three of them on our typical walk to Eastside Park and back. I enjoy the walks, but in this case I want to hurry back and get started. Sebastian has other ideas, walking at his typically glacial pace. I could measure his time in the forty-yard dash with a sundial.

When we finally get back, the phone is ringing. Laurie is in the kitchen and answers it. Moments later she comes to me with the phone. "It's for you."

"Who is it?"

"He wouldn't say, but I know who I hope it is."

That statement, plus the look on Laurie's face, pretty much eliminates the possibility that it's a telemarketer. I take the phone and decide to say the word that I have found to be an excellent conversation starter: "Hello?"

"Mr. Carpenter, I understand you've been looking for me."

"Who are you?"

"I . . . I'd rather not say."

"Then I have no idea if I'm looking for you."

"It's about Matt Reisinger."

"Then you've come to the right place. Thank you for getting in touch with me." I'm assuming that Samantha Reisinger reached him; there's no other way he could have known about me. "I have some questions to ask you. How—"

"I will meet with you, but only under my conditions."

"Name them."

"We meet where I say, just once, and that's it. We never talk again, and I never testify to anything."

I need to agree to everything he says; I can renegotiate later if the situation calls for it. "Agreed. But can I also ask some questions now?"

"No . . . I'm sorry." Then, "I have some documents for you."

"When can we meet?"

"Tomorrow. There's a place on Route Seventeen in Tuxedo, New York. It's abandoned now, but it used to be the Red Apple Rest Stop Restaurant."

"I know it." When I was a kid, my parents would take me on vacation trips to Monticello, and we would pass the place and sometimes stop there. It was sort of famous. "What time?"

"Nine P.M."

I'm about to point out that it will be dark then, but that might be the whole point. "I'll be there. How can I reach you if I need to?"

"You can't."

Click.

call the team together to discuss the phone call that I believe and hope was from Stephen Gilley.

The caller ID had said Private Caller, which is no proof of anything. If Gilley has been hiding for a long time, I wouldn't expect anything else.

My investigators have way more experience than I do in this area, so it's wise to get them together to plan our approach. Sam is here as well, since his expertise could be needed.

Laurie points out that it might not be Gilley, but someone hoping to lure me into a trap, for reasons unknown.

"Sorry, but I don't buy that," I say. "First of all, I haven't done anything that makes me worthy of trapping; at this point I'm not a danger to anyone but my client."

"The murderer might not see it that way," Laurie says. "You've been snooping around; it's possible that whoever we're dealing with has access to more information than we realize."

"That's not all," I say. "The person on the phone said that he knows I've been looking for him. Gilley is the only person I have been looking for, and the only person aware of it was Samantha Reisinger. She would not have told anyone else about this."

"I think you're right," Corey says. "But the best approach in situations like this is to act as if you're wrong and prepare for the worst. If it turns out you were correct, then no harm, no foul."

"Corey is right," Laurie says. "So unless Marcus disagrees, you're outvoted. The election wasn't even that close. Marcus?"

Marcus just nods; not even a grunt is necessary. Marcus voting with me against Laurie would be as unlikely as me beating Marcus in arm wrestling.

"Do I get a vote?" Sam asks.

"Depends. Are you voting with me or them?" I ask.

"Them."

"No vote for you," I say, mimicking the Soup Nazi in *Seinfeld*. No one seems to be in the mood for humor, so I move on. "I wasn't saying we shouldn't take precautions. I was just giving my opinion that this was really Gilley. The location also fits in with where Sam said he believed Gilley was located. He said the Monticello area, and this is on the way there."

"Good," Laurie says. "Then we agree. You'll meet with the guy, but we'll make sure that it's not a trap and that you stay safe."

Corey says, "My suggestion would be that Marcus and I go with you; I'll bring Simon as well. We'll scout out the area and move in if Gilley arrives and there are any concerns."

"Andy should also be wired so that you can hear what's going on, or he can call you. That way if there is any trouble once they start talking, you can intervene."

"I'll take care of that," Sam says.

"We'll get there before you," Corey says. "Actually, you can get near there around the same time; just don't approach the place until I call you and tell you it's clear."

I think they are being overly cautious, but I'm not going to argue the point. For one thing, there's no way they would listen to me. More important, as a coward I will like having them around when I enter the dark, abandoned rest stop.

The day goes by slowly, as its always done in these kinds of situations. I use part of the time to write Ricky a letter. I have no idea why, but it always seems awkward when I do so.

When Ricky is here, we talk endlessly and comfortably about a whole bunch of things, but when I start a letter, I have no idea what to say, and what I do say sounds stilted and strained.

It's about a forty-five-minute drive to Tuxedo, so we leave at seven o'clock. That should get us there an hour early, maybe a little later if there's any traffic. Corey, Marcus, and Simon Garfunkel go in Corey's car, and I follow them, even though I know where I'm going.

Laurie considered going also, but since some stealth is involved, she agreed that it was overkill. There is no question that Marcus, Corey, and Simon can handle any difficulties that may come up.

We pull into a McDonald's about a mile from the Red Apple. I'm going to wait here until I get the call from Corey that it's safe to go in. The way we have it set up, I should arrive before Gilley, but that doesn't matter either way. They will make sure that I'm safe however the chronology goes. Their plan is to make sure the area is secure, then enter the rest stop itself and confirm that there is no danger to me in place there.

I'm surprised when I get a call from Corey less than half an hour later. His message is short, sweet, but a bit ominous: "Get your ass in here."

pull up to the Red Apple, and for a moment I'm concerned when I don't see Corey's car.

It briefly crosses my mind that they could have been forced to call me in, but then I realize that we're talking about Marcus. No one forces Marcus to do anything, and Corey is no slouch either. Then there's Simon Garfunkel, a great dog who would tear the arm off anyone threatening Corey.

They no doubt parked elsewhere to avoid being seen. I wouldn't expect them to be inside either, since that was not the plan. But something about the way Corey said I should get my "ass in here" led me to believe they were inside.

I'm a little nervous about entering, but I have no choice, so I open the door and enter the abandoned building. There is still some daylight, but it's fading rapidly. It's considerably darker inside, and the whole situation is made more creepy as the floorboards creak as I walk.

Corey's voice calls out from somewhere toward the back of the building. "We're back here. Hurry up, Andy."

I push open a door that seems to lead toward the sound of his voice. Ten feet ahead there's another door, and I think I see a light behind it, so I go through that one. Sure enough, there are people back here, holding two flashlights.

When my eyes adjust, I can see that Corey, Marcus, Simon,

and a man I assume must be Gilley are present. Of the four of them, only Corey, Marcus, and Simon are conscious, at least that's the way it appears. Gilley is lying on the floor; I can't see well enough to tell his condition.

"I think your meeting has been called off," Corey says, and he shines his flashlight on the body, which up until now had only been slightly illuminated by reflected light.

I have seen a number of disgustingly gory sights, far more than they ever predicted in law school, that's for sure. But this is among the worst. Suffice it to say that someone used a knife on him and did not do so with surgical precision.

"Holy shit. He was like this when you got here?"

"Obviously," Corey says. "But he wasn't killed here. Simon found the scene, about fifty yards out in those woods. He was dragged in here and left this way."

"Why would they do that?"

"To send you a message," Corey says. "They wanted you to find him and see what they are capable of. It was set up this way to scare you."

"Mission accomplished," I say. "Do we know for sure that it's Gilley?"

"No, he had no identification on him; they probably took it. And of course the documents he said he was bringing are gone as well."

"Did you call the cops?"

Corey doesn't have to answer; the sounds of approaching sirens do the job for him. But he says, "I have a friend in the New York State Police, a captain named Johnny Everton. He's stationed not far from here, so I contacted him. I wanted to make sure they knew who they were dealing with when they arrived."

Within a few minutes, flashlights are no longer necessary. Floodlights on the arriving cars turn the area into bright daylight; the Red Apple has not seen this much action in a long time.

The cops come in, in force, guns drawn and yelling for no one to move. We're not about to. The cop that seems to be in charge looks over and says, "Hey, Corey," and for the first time since they arrived, I exhale. Corey responds with "Hey, John," and we're all buddies.

Captain Everton takes in the entire scene and then says to us, "You guys know who this is?"

"We think we do," Corey says. "Name is Stephen Gilley. He's from Cincinnati, but we think he was living in the Monticello area."

"Any chance you know who did this to him?"

Corey shakes his head. "That's a negative. But it wasn't done here; it was done in the woods back there and the body was dragged inside."

"Why?"

"That's a long story," I say.

Everton smiles. "I want to hear every word of it."

Laurie calls a friend in Paterson PD who is accomplished in such matters and asks him to check our phones at home to make sure they are not tapped.

He comes out immediately with two fellow officers, and they determine in just a few minutes that we're clean. It's a relief; I would hate to think that I did something to cause Gilley's horrible death.

Of course, the unpleasant truth is I really did cause his death by stirring up these events from years ago. He had successfully hidden from these people for years until Andy Carpenter came along. Even though I was just doing my job and certainly had no way of knowing that the killers were lying in wait for Gilley, I am going to feel the guilt for quite a while.

I call Samantha Reisinger, but I don't tell her what has happened. I see no reason to at this point; it would only cause her pain and guilt and might also scare the hell out of her. I do ask if she has had any issues with her phone lately, falsely claiming that I was having trouble reaching her.

She tells me that, yes, a man from the phone company was out yesterday checking the lines. I have no doubt that her phone was tapped, and that is how the killers knew where Gilley was going to be. They must also have been watching when I arrived at Samantha's house, which prompted the wiretap.

These people are careful and well financed, and they are good at what they do.

I can add not telling her about Gilley to the things I feel bad about because Samantha has a right to know what happened. I rationalize it by knowing that nothing will bring her husband back, and that I am doing this to find his killer.

But I do not want her freaking out and going to the media with this; I have to manage the timeline better. And it's not like she isn't going to find out about Gilley; the police will just be the ones to tell her.

I'm exhausted this morning; we were in Tuxedo until 1:00 A.M. giving our statements, first to Everton, and then we had additional questioning by a homicide cop. Fortunately we were not treated as suspects, no doubt because of Corey's relationship with Everton.

The one positive in this, if a vicious and horrible murder can include a positive, is that there is no longer any doubt that what we have been pursuing is real.

None of this is a coincidence. Reisinger was, in fact, murdered. And Gilley's death was related to it, almost certainly committed by people in the same conspiracy. There is no way that a killer just happened to be hanging out at the abandoned Red Apple Rest, waiting for someone to wander by. Gilley was killed because he was going to supply information about Reisinger's death, and about what was the ultimate motive for it.

I also know, not factually but in my gut, that the other deaths in the companies owned by Wasserman Equities were all related and were all murders. Philip Callan did not chug down some peanuts and forget his two EpiPens as he walked through the park that night, that's for damn sure.

Laurie and Corey are looking into the other deaths in the

Wasserman companies, and I would bet that we will come to the same conclusion about at least some of them.

There are many things we don't yet know, and three of those things are all-important. We don't know why these homicides have taken place, we don't know what is going on at Wasserman Equities, and we, meaning I, have no idea how to get any of this in front of a jury.

I'm taking it on faith that what Robbie Divine intimated, and Corey Douglas learned, about Wasserman Equities being financed with dirty money is true. And it's possible that Rachel knew about that through her husband, and when he died, she resolved to do something about it.

That makes sense.

What doesn't make sense, unfortunately, is that these executives of Wasserman-owned companies would be killed because of it. Once Wasserman bought their companies, the source of the money would cease to be relevant.

People like Reisinger would have cashed out from the sale and gotten even richer than they had been. Where Wasserman got the money to buy them out would never come up once the sale was completed. And it also shouldn't affect the ongoing operations of the companies; no matter who was behind the money, or behind Wasserman Equities, they would want the acquired companies to be run efficiently and profitably.

Samantha Reisinger said that her husband was troubled and stressed by what was happening at his company, Global Aviation. Stephen Gilley knew what that was and, like his boss, paid for it with his life. It is entirely possible, in fact likely, that Philip Callan and other executives of their companies met their fate for similar reasons.

We have to find out what those reasons were.

I call Lieutenant Anthony, the Ohio police officer that I spoke to about Reisinger. He asked me to advise him if I had any updates to share, and I'm doing that now.

"What have you got for me?" he asks.

"Matt Reisinger was murdered."

"I thought we went over that in my office. You got any more evidence now than you had then?"

"No, but I have another murder that was committed to cover it up."

"I'm listening."

I tell him about my conversation with Samantha Reisinger and about Stephen Gilley and her belief that he knew the truth. Then I say, "I think she contacted him and told him to call me."

"And did he?"

"Yeah, we were supposed to meet last night. But someone got to him first. They tortured and killed him."

"Where was this?"

"Tuxedo, New York. You can google the story; it's hit the media. He had been on the run and afraid of these people for years, ever since Reisinger got pushed over that cliff. I told the NY State Police all about Reisinger, and I gave them your name, so I'm sure they'll be contacting you."

"If what you're saying is true, this puts a new spin on things."

"No shit, Sherlock. In the meantime, you might want to check Samantha Reisinger's phone. I'm sure the bad guys have tapped it, or whatever you do to phones these days. It's the only way they could have found out where Gilley was supposed to meet me. And she said a guy from the phone company stopped by to check the line."

"Why was Gilley willing to talk to you and not us?" Anthony asks, a perfectly logical question.

"Maybe he thought you wouldn't believe him, like you didn't believe Samantha Reisinger. Maybe he was afraid that whoever killed Reisinger would find out and kill him also. Seems like a reasonable assumption at this point."

"But why would he tell you?"

"Maybe he thought he could trust me, and that we were far enough away that the bad guys wouldn't find out. Or maybe he finally wanted his life back."

"Didn't work out so well."

"No, it didn't. That's something I'll have to live with."

My next call is to Sam, to tell him I have a crash assignment for him and the entire team. "I want you to look at everything concerning Global Aviation. They're a Wasserman company based in Cincinnati."

"I know. I told you about them and Reisinger in the first place."

"So you did."

"What is it you want us to find out?"

"I'm looking to understand their business. Where they fly, who they fly, and when. I'm looking for inconsistencies, anything that jumps out at you as strange. Or maybe there are consistencies that make no sense."

"So bottom line, you're floundering around with no idea what you're looking for."

"Exactly. So find it."

My final call is to Gerald Bridges, the reporter who works for Vince and was dealing with Rachel Morehouse. "I've got a story for you."

I can almost see him smile through the phone. "That's what I'm here for."

I tell him about my involvement in the murder at the Red Apple, and I cryptically tell him that it relates to the Tony Wasserman case. The money quote from me is "The real murderers are out there, while Tony Wasserman sits unfairly accused in jail."

"Perfect," he says. "It will be in tomorrow's paper, and online tonight. Vince will owe you one for this."

"I think you're confusing Vince with someone who has a shred of human decency."

"You're right. My mistake."

I take the dogs for their morning walk, and I use the time to decide my approach to a meeting I have this afternoon.

Carl Simmons finally called and was willing to talk to me, after fending me off all this time. Simmons is the co-CEO with Jim Wolford at Wasserman Equities. I have a much different view of that company than I did when I met Wolford, so I'll use a different strategy.

I discuss my plans with Tara, who is able to multitask. She can sniff her surroundings and listen to me at the same time. Hunter seems interested as well, because anything Tara does Hunter approves of. Sebastian couldn't care less; he just wants to get home and go to sleep.

I head home to get ready for a court appearance this morning. Judge Lofton has summoned the lawyers to a hearing, which I'm sure is a result of the story about Gilley that I placed in Vince's paper. I'm going to get reprimanded; it's like I'm being sent to the principal's office.

When I left the house with the dogs, only Laurie was there. That has changed substantially during my absence; Corey and Marcus are now here as well. They all seem to be waiting for me, and they ask me to sit down with them in the den. I do so warily; this is how it must feel to walk into an intervention.

"What's going on, team?"

"You need to be protected," Laurie says with uncharacteristic bluntness.

"Just like that? You usually beat around the bush for a while, and we discuss it."

She nods. "I considered that, but rejected it. It always starts to feel like a negotiation, and this is not negotiable."

"Just who is it I need to be protected from?" I ask, though I know the answer.

"That's part of the problem; we don't know. But you saw what the danger is the other night. I don't want that to happen to you; the last thing I want to do is have to reenter the dating scene."

"You'd spend your life vainly searching for someone as good as me."

"Maybe."

"Look, I know there are dangerous people involved here, but I don't see the danger to me. They knew I was coming there to meet Gilley; they could have tried to kill me at the same time."

Corey says, "This was step one; they were sending you a message. Otherwise Gilley's body would have been left in the woods, or more likely buried and never found."

"And the message was to back off," Laurie says. "But you won't do that; you can't do that. So at some point, if you make progress, they are going to decide that you are more trouble than you're worth."

"What about if I don't make progress? That seems to be the direction this is headed."

"Andy . . ." She doesn't have to finish the sentence; the meaning is clear just by the way she says my name. She's not in the mood to argue.

I've run into this situation a number of times, mainly because Laurie has little respect for my self-protection abilities. I always face the same quandary: I want to be protected, but I don't want to admit that I want to be protected.

Fortunately, Laurie couldn't care less what I want. "Andy, the only debate about this, and it has already taken place, is whether we should protect you with or without you knowing about it. We've obviously decided to go with telling you. Don't make us regret it."

"So this is where Marcus comes in?" I ask.

Laurie nods. "This is where Marcus comes in. You know the drill; just go about your business. If you have any difficulty, Marcus will be there to deal with it. Marcus?"

Marcus nods. "Yunhh."

"One other thing; you'll be wearing a wire whenever you're out of the house. Marcus will be on the other end; if you need him, you just have to say the word. It's also set up to record, so don't say anything embarrassing."

"What about my privacy?"

"Your constitutional right to privacy has been suspended for the duration of this case," Laurie says.

Corey says, "Okay, that's settled. Now let us tell you what Laurie and I have learned about the other incidents involving executives at companies owned by Wasserman Equities.

"Shawna Beasley, thirty-eight, was the chief financial officer at Chilton Manufacturing, based in Louisville, but with six factories in four states. They make a variety of things, companies hire them on three-to-five-year contracts. Lately they have been making toys, garden equipment, and power hand tools.

"Beasley left the company, though the circumstances behind her departure are not clear. She definitely had a problem with the new management and was escorted out of the building. She died three weeks later in a motorcycle crash. The police ruled the death accidental."

Laurie says, "As the CFO, she might have had special insight into the source of what we think was dirty money."

Corey nods and continues, "Arnold Etheridge, seventy-one, was the CEO of National Trucking Inc., obviously a trucking and shipping company. They were also available for contract hire and worked throughout the United States and Canada, but were based in Minneapolis.

"Etheridge died of a sudden heart attack while out jogging. He'd had a triple bypass three years earlier, so the death was not a total surprise. His wife did not suspect any kind of foul play and therefore did not request an autopsy."

"And your opinion?" I ask.

"When you couple it with what we already know, it stinks. Obviously the heart attack could have been murder, we know that from Rachel Morehouse. The hit-and-run is clearly foul play."

"One thing bothers me about Rachel's killing, which I just realized," I say.

"What's that?" Laurie asks.

"It was sloppy. We're dealing with professionals who haven't made a mistake. The only reason we knew what really happened to Gilley is that they wanted us to. But Rachel's case was different. The bruises on her wrists, the needle mark . . . if not for that there would not have been an autopsy, and we wouldn't be sitting here."

"So what do you take from that?" Laurie asks.

"I don't have the slightest idea."

The hearing is in Judge Lofton's chambers, with me, Kathryn Strickland, and a court reporter also present.

It's at the courthouse in Hackensack because the trial is in Bergen County. It's not terribly convenient for me, and I have to remember to allow more time to get there. Judges aren't crazy about lawyers who are late. Actually, judges aren't crazy about lawyers at all.

I've never met this judge; I came on to the case after the arraignment. But based on his expression, he already dislikes me. That's unusual; ordinarily it takes a meeting and a conversation or two for judges to dislike me, and then another meeting for them to detest me. It generally goes further downhill from there, but it's a process.

As I sit down, I realize to my total horror that I am still wearing the wire; I forgot to take it off. If Judge Lofton finds out I am wearing a wire in his chambers, by the end of the day Laurie will be bailing me out, and I'll be wearing an electronic ankle bracelet in addition to the wire.

"The reason for this hearing being called is the story that broke in the media this morning," he says, which is not a surprise. "Mr. Carpenter, I assume you acknowledge that you were the source of the story?"

"If by that Your Honor is asking if I was interviewed for the story, and whether or not my quote is accurate, then the answer to both questions is yes."

"That is exactly what I am asking. And now I am telling you that this is unacceptable."

I feign puzzlement. I'm often puzzled, so learning to feign it was easy. "I wasn't aware that Your Honor had issued an order forbidding contact with the press."

"Contact with the press is one thing. A deliberate attempt to taint the jury pool is another."

I have never met a jury pool I wasn't happy to taint, but I don't think I will mention that. "Your Honor, the reporter asked me a question and I answered it honestly. I also answered it accurately."

"You also answered it improperly, Mr. Carpenter. Your reputation precedes you; do not let it define you in my courtroom."

Now he's pissing me off. While I admit my courtroom style is unconventional, and judges recoil from it, I think I'm considered a damn good lawyer who fights for my clients. It's time to establish some ground rules here and show that I can't be pushed around.

"Your Honor, when my client was arrested, Ms. Strickland and her boss held a press conference to announce it. I was not aware then, nor am I aware now, of any necessity to have done so.

"No public interest was served in having that press conference. The public was not living in fear that a crazed killer with hypodermics filled with potassium chloride was terrorizing New Jersey. That press conference was an obvious attempt to taint the jury pool, but if the prosecution was reprimanded, I missed the meeting."

Judge Lofton turns away from me for the first time. "Ms. Strickland?"

"Your Honor, a press conference like that in a case with this media attention is standard procedure."

"Your Honor, Ms. Strickland and I will likely not agree on much in this case, but on this we do agree. Attempting to taint the jury pool is standard procedure for the prosecution."

"That is nonsense," she says.

Judge Lofton frowns his annoyance. "I will be issuing a gag order this afternoon, prohibiting all contact with the press on this matter. Violations will result in severe sanctions. Does everyone understand?"

Strickland and I both say that we do in fact understand, and Judge Lofton dismisses us. Once we're out of his chambers, she smiles and repeats his comment: "Your reputation precedes you."

I return the smile. "I don't know who he has been talking to. I'm actually widely loved."

In anticipation of my meeting with Carl Simmons, I call Sam Willis to set up something that has worked well for us in the past.

"Talk to me," Sam says, as always answering the phone on the first ring.

"Sam, can you get Carl Simmons's cell phone number?"

"Duh." He's insulted by the question. Sam could get the queen of England's cell phone number if he wanted it, although I doubt she would take his call.

"Good. I'm meeting with him at three o'clock this afternoon. If I'm right, he'll throw me out of his office by three oh five. But in any event, starting at three, I want to know who he calls."

"What if he makes calls from his office phone? It would be impossible to trace which of the employees made the calls."

"I understand. But if he's planning on saying anything incriminating, he would more likely use his cell phone, so the switchboard operator or anyone else couldn't listen in. Anyway, it's worth a shot."

"I'm on it." Sam's ability to tap into the phone company computers to track calls and GPS locations is invaluable.

In this case I am going in obviously already distrustful of Simmons. If bad things are going on at Wasserman-owned companies, then he and Jim Wolford, as heads of the company, are prime suspects to be behind them.

I arrive at Wasserman Equities promptly at 3:00 P.M., and I am told that Mr. Simmons is in a meeting that is running late, so I should have a seat and will be informed when he is ready.

I sit down and pick a *Sports Illustrated* from the magazine rack. It's the current issue, which is a rarity in waiting rooms. I wish their magazine person would go to work for my dentist.

The elevator door opens and Jim Wolford steps out with two other men. They're talking as they walk by; I'm sure Wolford sees me, but he doesn't acknowledge me in any way. I don't think I'm as loved here as I used to be.

At a quarter past three I'm called in to see Simmons. He's not in his office, but actually walks in right behind me. No smile, no offer of a handshake, no indication that we're buddies.

He walks around and takes a seat behind his desk. It's large, with a glass top, close to the size of the conference table in my office. It also has nothing on it, not even a phone or a computer. I have no idea what he does behind this thing all day.

"I read where you had an interesting time the other night?" It's a statement, but he makes it sound like a question.

"I did."

"And you said it had something to do with the Rachel Morehouse case?"

"I did."

"You want to tell me what you meant by that?"

"Hey, this is great. Usually I have to keep meetings like this moving along, but with you asking the questions, I don't have that burden. Later, when I get you on the witness stand, I'll be asking the questions. That will be a different kind of fun."

He smiles, but not exactly warmly. "Good, then answer the question."

"Okay, but it's sort of a long answer; try and keep up. Matt Reisinger . . . you know him, right?"

"I did. He was a good man."

"The operative word being *was*. He was murdered, pushed off a cliff."

"I believe it was ruled an accidental death."

"Which was an incorrect ruling. Anyway, we're getting off the track here. Stephen Gilley, the man who was killed the other night, knew the circumstances behind Reisinger's death. He told me some of it, and we were going to talk some more. The killers found out about it and intervened."

"What does this have to do with me?"

"Well, it turns out, and this is the damnedest thing, but Matt Reisinger isn't the only murder victim who worked for you. Your employees don't do well on the actuarial tables; do you offer combat pay?"

"I don't know what you are talking about."

"Which part was confusing? I'm here to help."

"You have actual evidence to back up these accusations? Or is this just some more lawyer bullshit?"

"It's both, but I'm going to wait to present the evidence in court. You'll be there to hear it."

"Time for you to leave."

"Really?" I look at my watch. "Boy, time flies when you're having fun."

I head down to the jail basically for no other reason than to let Tony know he hasn't been forgotten. It obviously can be lonely there, and it's important for him to know that we are working hard to get him the hell out.

When I get there, I'm pleasantly surprised to see Eddie Dowd is already here. He and Tony have developed a friendship during the case preparation, which pleases me greatly.

So basically I just say hello and I get the hell out of here. And I make a note to thank Eddie for being a good guy.

Stal was not surprised when he got the call. The message was clear; Carpenter was not going away. At least not voluntarily.

So what they needed to do in response was also clear, and Stal immediately took the step necessary to make it happen.

He called the man who went by the name Chris Marrero and instructed him to return to Philadelphia. Marrero had been in his Detroit home, not sure whether Stal would call. First of all, no action might have been needed at all; Stal had pointed that out. Second, even if Stal decided that action was necessary, Marrero might not have been the choice to make it happen. It could have been Roy Callison.

Obviously, the method Stal had chosen was one that required one of Marrero's unique talents. He and Callison complemented each other; between them there was pretty much nothing they could not do.

Once again, Stal did not mince words. Carpenter was to be dealt with, and time was of the essence. Marrero didn't know why, and he certainly didn't ask. He knew the drill; he was paid a lot of money to do his job and to not question orders.

When Stal told him the method, Marrero was surprised. Usually these jobs required stealth and deception. Murders were to be committed in such a way that they were not even recognized as murders.

Not this time.

Stal knew that Marrero had to be surprised about what Stal was saying, but he did not consider telling Marrero the reasons for these decisions.

Stal did not share a number of things. While the murder of Carpenter would raise uncomfortable questions, that was not the important consideration. Timing was the key here; Carpenter was making noise and calling attention to things that couldn't survive the sunlight. He had to be stopped now before others climbed on the bandwagon.

Any difficulties brought on by his death could likely be handled. It might result in changes at the top of the American operation, but these people were puppets that could be replaced.

It was of no concern to Stal what happened in the trial of Morehouse's stepson. Carpenter's death would certainly result in a mistrial; he knew enough about the American system to be sure of that. And maybe it would create enough doubt that Wasserman would ultimately be acquitted. Stal could not care less about any of that.

But the elimination of Carpenter would buy time, and that was all they needed. They didn't even need much of it; almost all the pieces were already in place. They had taken root, and they would grow until they were called upon to act. Soon, or next year, or the year after that.

Marrero didn't need to know any of that.

Stal was calling the shots.

Literally.

My goal for the meeting was to piss Carl Simmons off . . . mission accomplished.

My other goal was to scare him, but the jury is still out on that. I'm sure Simmons is a smart guy, and he would know that if I had anything to cause him a major problem, he would have been questioned by the police instead of me. I'll know better when I hear from Sam about any calls Simmons might have made after I left.

I had no qualms about confronting him directly. If he is really involved in a conspiracy, then he knows about my visit to Cincinnati, and he certainly knows about Gilley and why he was killed. For all I know he ordered the killing.

If he's not involved in the conspiracy, then it doesn't matter to me what he thinks or does.

Today's attempt to get somewhere, anywhere, brings me to Special Agent Carol Bracey, assigned to the Organized Crime division of the FBI, based in Newark. Our friend Cindy Spodek, herself an agent, working in Boston, set it up.

If dirty money was behind Wasserman and now his successors, and if laundering that money is worth committing multiple murders, it might be nice to know the source of that money.

I have to get through three layers of security before I actually get to Agent Bracey's office. Apparently the FBI would prefer that terrorists not be able to get inside their buildings, and I'm not so sure they're thrilled about lawyers being here either.

"Thanks for seeing me," I say.

"Cindy Spodek has been an important mentor to me." That is another way of Bracey's saying that if it wasn't for Cindy, I wouldn't have gotten through security. "So you want to talk about Wasserman Equities?"

I had told Cindy the purpose of the meeting, and she obviously conveyed it to Bracey.

"Yes."

"What about them?"

"I have reason to believe that they were funded by money that was somewhat less than clean, supplied by people who hoped that it would be effectively laundered when it came out the other side."

"Wouldn't be the first time."

"I'm sure that's true, but is there any information you could provide that is specific to them?"

"I haven't been involved with them, but I looked into it. I'm afraid I came up empty. There have been some rumors over the years, but that's true with a lot of companies. Nothing was ever discovered to confirm them, and the available information didn't rise to the level of starting a formal investigation. You could check with the SEC, but I suspect you'll get the same response."

"Is laundering money common with these kinds of companies?"

"I wouldn't say common, no. But it happens. The key is to get the money into the system. It then becomes hard, if not impossible, to trace and distinguish from legitimate money."

"Is there any way for me to trace it?"

"Not really . . . not at this point. You'd have to get witnesses to testify to their knowledge of it. You can imagine how difficult that would be. How much money are we talking about?"

"In the last five years they have spent eleven billion dollars on acquisitions."

She frowns. "It's very unlikely that kind of money could be involved and not come onto our radar with flashing red lights. Organized crime is not that successful an industry these days."

This is not the kind of thing I like to hear. "What's the goal once the money is put into the system?"

She shrugs. "Just like any other investor. Once it's clean, they want it to earn more. So they would want the businesses they bought to be successful, so they could be operated or sold off at a profit."

I thank Bracey and leave. It was a singularly unsuccessful meeting, but at least I got to see Newark.

On the way home I call Sam and ask him if he traced any calls from Simmons's phone.

"There were two. At three thirty-five he called his partner, James Wolford, at his home. They talked for seven minutes."

"And the other one?"

"He called a phone not listed in anyone's name; it must have been a burner phone."

"Can you tell where that phone was when he called it? Or where it is now?"

"Negative. The GPS was deactivated, and the phone has been turned off or destroyed. I would imagine you are dealing with people who know what they're doing."

This has turned into another nonevent. Simmons could have been calling Wolford for any of a thousand good reasons. I was hoping that Simmons, in a panic, had called Organized Crime

Inc. and spoken to their customer service division. But he hadn't. He called his partner, maybe to discuss buying another company with dirty money we can't trace.

The trial is bearing down on us and we are mostly defenseless. Since I'm a defense attorney, that's not where I need to be.

As so often happens, the idea comes to me while I'm walking the dogs.

I'm not sure why that is . . . maybe picking up dog shit clears the mind. But as soon as I get home, I call Eddie Dowd and ask him to immediately prepare a request to the court to have Stanley Wasserman's body exhumed, and to file it as urgent. I also tell him that he needs to go down to the jail and get a signed request from Tony to have it done.

Rachel Morehouse and Stanley Wasserman both died of sudden heart attacks. Rachel's death was determined to be a murder, but Stanley never had an autopsy. Rachel just assumed it was a natural death and exercised her right not to have the medical examiner step in.

But if Rachel was murdered, was Stanley? It's certainly possible, and if it turns out to be the case, the information would be at least partially exculpatory for Tony.

I tell Laurie what I am doing, and she thinks it's a good idea. "How do you get it done?" she asks.

"We get Tony to request it; as the son he has the right to do so. Once the court approves it, we get some shovels and start digging, metaphorically."

"Even in Tony's current position, the court will honor the request?"

"We'll find that out soon enough."

"What about Arnold Etheridge, the Minnesota trucking executive who died of a heart attack as well? Should you try and do the same for him?"

"Excellent idea; we would just go through the same process, this time with his wife making the request. Can you call her? I don't know if you've noticed, but you have more of a way with people than I do."

"Sure. I'll just start with 'You don't know me, but I want to dig up your dead husband.'"

"Perfect. But say it with more charm than that."

I drive out to Upper Saddle River, where I have a meeting scheduled with Brooke Schlosser, a neighbor of Rachel's, though the term *neighbor* in that area has to be used loosely. Schlosser lives just two houses away, but that represents almost a quarter of a mile.

The Schlosser house, while impressive by any normal standard, could serve as Rachel's guesthouse. It is probably half the size and also seems to be sitting on a much-smaller piece of property. It has a long driveway and a swimming pool, but, horror of horrors, only has one tennis court.

I need to organize a benefit for these people.

Schlosser is the neighbor who reported hearing a loud argument between Rachel and Tony the morning of her death. She greets me politely and offers me coffee, which I accept, but I sense a wariness about her. I think she sees me as the enemy; she has cast her lot with the prosecution.

I have trouble seeing her as the enemy, though, since she has a gorgeous golden retriever named Cheyenne, who sits next to me and graciously lets me pet her head the entire time we're talking. Cheyenne is obviously loved and well cared for . . . point for Brooke Schlosser.

"I was walking Cheyenne that morning as I always do; we do

a couple of miles and then come home the back way," she says. "So we went past Rachel's house on the way. I always stopped by to see if she wanted to join me with Lion. Cheyenne loves Lion."

"Everybody loves Lion."

"Is he okay?" Yet another point for her.

"He's fine, believe me. So you walked up the driveway towards her house?"

"Yes, there was a car in the driveway, which I assumed was Tony's, though I don't know that for sure. Anyway, as I got close, I heard yelling. One of the voices was Rachel's, and the other was Tony's."

"You knew Tony?"

"Oh, yes. I met him a couple of times at Rachel's. We all had lunch together one time."

"Did they get along well, in your view?"

She nods. "I think so, or at least I thought so until that day. Rachel never said otherwise."

"Could you hear what they said during the argument?"

"Not really . . . just that they were angry. They were yelling over each other; it was hard to make out."

"So you never went in?"

"No, it would have been uncomfortable. I just went back down the driveway and walked Cheyenne the rest of the way."

"But you're sure the voice was Tony's?

"I'm positive. I wouldn't say so otherwise."

Sam is waiting for me when I get home; Laurie has been feeding him pretzels and pistachios while he waits. I'm always happy to see Sam show up unannounced; it means he has good, or at least interesting, news to report.

On the rare occasions that he comes up empty, he usually calls to tell me so. When he's got something, he likes to get the praise in person.

"So we looked into Global Aviation," he says, once he's swallowed all the pretzels. "They are a charter company that mostly flies individuals both domestically and internationally. As you might expect, most of their clients are businesses that want private travel for their top executives."

So far he hasn't told me anything I didn't already know, so all I can do is wait. He will get to the good stuff.

"If you're a private client, what you effectively do is take an ownership interest in a plane . . . let's say you buy one sixty-fourth of it. Then you have the right to use it for a certain number of hours per month, or year, as the case may be. You're not always using the same plane, but if not, it's one of equal size."

Eventually Sam will get to what I want to hear, if I can only be patient. I can see that Laurie is about thirty seconds from pulling every hair out of her head.

"But what I found interesting is the international operation. They don't average more than three or four flights a month, and always from Portugal."

"So?"

"So they always leave at the same time, and the flight plan shows that they will arrive at Newark Airport at ten fifteen P.M., every time. But here's the thing, they are always fifty-five minutes late. They get there at eleven ten, without fail. You can set your watch by it."

"Interesting," I say, because it is. "Anything else?"

"Yes. The logs show that the plane is always empty, no passengers. It's apparently listed as a return trip, just bringing the plane back to this country."

"But it's not?"

"I can't say for sure, but I can't find any trips where the plane went over there in the first place. How can the plane return if it never left?"

It's an excellent question, and one worth all the pretzels and pistachios that Sam can suck down. Before he leaves, I ask him if he has access to the flight plans before the planes take off.

"Of course. Why do you insult me?"

"Sorry, I want to know when Global Aviation's next flight is scheduled to leave Portugal."

He nods.

When he leaves, I ask Laurie what she thinks is going on, but she has just as little an idea as I do. I assign her and her team the job of figuring it out, working with Sam.

"If you come up with something," I say, "it's all the pretzels you can eat."

This is my second hearing before Judge Lofton; unfortunately it won't be long before I'm seeing him every day.

Kathryn Strickland has asked for the session to lodge an objection to our efforts to exhume Stanley Wasserman's body. That she has done so is a sign of how hard-fought the trial is going to be.

This time the hearing is in the courtroom, not in Judge Lofton's chambers. The public is not here, but Eddie Dowd is with me; he has filed our brief stating our position.

I have also arranged for Tony to be here. He has the right to attend, and I might call on him to speak, though I doubt it. Either way, it's a chance for him to get out of his cell and stretch his legs.

Judge Lofton starts it off by saying, "Ms. Strickland, you have lodged an objection to the request to exhume the body of Stanley Wasserman. I have your brief, but please state your objection verbally."

She stands. She has a good presence about her and the ability to command a courtroom, even one that has no jury and no people in the gallery.

"Thank you, Your Honor. We certainly object to this request. It is obviously the first salvo by the defense to introduce irrelevant information and muddy the waters in our upcoming trial.

It is a continuation of the media efforts that Your Honor condemned, in that Mr. Carpenter is intent on going on a fishing expedition. He is throwing the first lines into the water, in his hope to convince this court to admit what should properly be inadmissible.

"We are here to find the facts behind the murder of Rachel Morehouse. We do not need to literally dig up unrelated and irrelevant matters. Stanley Wasserman died of a heart attack; no foul play was alleged then, and none is alleged now, except by a desperate defense. They make no offer of proof that Mr. Wasserman's death was anything other than of natural causes."

The judge turns to me. "Mr. Carpenter? I assume you disagree with that assessment?"

"Of course, Your Honor. But even more than that, I am amazed by it. The prosecution has just said that they have analyzed our future strategy, and because they disagree with it, they want to preemptively stop us from executing it.

"They have no idea what our strategy is, and the truth is that at this point it's none of their business. We have not attempted to interfere with their case; they should not interfere with ours.

"And most remarkable is how little respect they show for Your Honor's ability to control this courtroom and this trial. When the time comes to present our case, you will decide what is admissible and what isn't. Whether or not we have exhumed Mr. Wasserman's body is not the point; the point is that you will examine the available facts and make a ruling. Ms. Strickland's apparent belief that we can pressure you to come down with a ruling favorable to our side is . . . well, I wish it were true, but we both know it isn't.

"Lastly, at this moment the exhumation request has nothing to do with this trial. I admit that it might at some future point, but right now it doesn't. It is a perfectly legitimate request, and the truth is we could have filed it in a different court had we so chosen. But we wanted to be transparent, never expecting that the prosecution would be so desperate to control the defense case that they would object."

Strickland spends almost the entire time I am talking shaking her head. "Your Honor, Mr. Carpenter would have us believe that this might have nothing to do with our case? That his asking for the exhumation of the late husband of our victim, and the father of our defendant, is a total coincidence? I would respectfully say that is nonsense; he is building a case on smoke and mirrors and asking Your Honor to give it a premature blessing."

Now it's my turn to shake my head. "Your Honor, Ms. Strickland misstates my position, which is disappointing, since I just stated it moments ago. I clearly said that the exhumation information might relate to our case at some future point.

"But the relevant fact is that it is Tony Wasserman's right to make this request and have it honored. I would submit that his motives for doing so are irrelevant. And I would ask, Who is harmed by granting the request? The interests of justice might be served, or the result may prove to be meaningless, but so what? Certainly no one will be damaged in the process."

Judge Lofton says that he will consider the matter and post his ruling later on the court website. I think he is not ruling from the bench because he doesn't want me to be present for my victory, because there is no way he can rule against us.

If he did, I could go to another courthouse and secure a positive ruling. We are in the right, even if Strickland is right about our motives.

And she certainly is.

This time Susan Wolford and I don't sit in her sitting room. Instead she suggests we sit outside by her pool, pointing out that it's a rare cool day. I have to admit that it's nice being out here. I'm not usually an outside, lay-in-the-sun kind of guy, but give me this setup and a piña colada and I could make do.

"They've told me I've got to testify. I'm very nervous about it," she says, once we've finished about three minutes of excruciating small talk. I feel sorry for Marcus, who is lurking somewhere nearby listening to this gibberish on the wire Sam placed on me.

"You'll be fine; nothing to be nervous about. You just tell the truth as you know it. You won't be on the stand long."

"You'll be asking me questions too?"

"Probably. Just like I did last time we met, and I'm doing now. The only difference is that you'll be under oath and people will be watching."

She smiles nervously. "Go easy on me."

"I'll do my best. Last time I was here, you told me that you saw Rachel the morning that she died."

"Yes."

"What time was that?"

"About ten thirty. I know that because I went directly from the gym, and I had a session with my trainer that ended at ten."

"Was Tony in the house?"

"I assume so."

"What makes you say that?"

"A couple of times, when we were talking about Tony, Rachel talked softly, almost whispered. She said she didn't want him to hear."

"She was saying negative things about him?"

"No, not really. She liked him. She was just saying that things were not going as well as she had hoped, that he was being cold and distant."

This does not track with Tony's assessment, or with Tony's feelings about Rachel. But different people see things differently, and it's possible that Rachel saw it the way Susan is describing.

"You drove there that morning?"

"Of course."

"Was there another car in the driveway when you pulled in?"

She thinks for a moment. "No, I don't think so."

"Did Rachel tell you why she wanted to be active in the business? I mean, considering how ill she was and how she might not have had a lot of time left?"

Susan shakes her head. "No, she didn't, and I would never ask. Because of Jim being there, it was an area we didn't get into. We were good friends, but I just didn't feel comfortable crossing that line."

"Did her involvement surprise you?"

"I didn't think much about it, but in retrospect, I guess it does."

"Did it surprise your husband?"

"Yes, I think so, but he was fine with it. He liked Rachel; we all liked Rachel."

This is going to answer the age-old question: If money and murder are involved, is there anything the media won't cover?

Laurie and I are at the Glen View Cemetery in Tenafly. It would be a lovely scene, with rolling hills and perfectly manicured grass, if not for what looks like thousands of headstones, each sitting above a dead person.

Stanley Wasserman is buried here, alongside his parents, Charles and Miriam Wasserman. There is plenty of room for Rachel as well, but she's not here yet, and I'm not sure why.

There is actually enough room for an entire platoon of Wassermans, should the need arise. Stanley and his parents are in what seems to be a spot of privilege, with trees providing shade and plenty of distance separating them from the other "permanent residents."

I assume this is what money can buy when there remains no time left to spend it.

The media are camped at the entrance to the grounds; there must be thirty reporters and cameramen. There is nothing for them to see, and no results are going to be learned or reported today.

I have no idea what they think they are accomplishing by being here, or how they will convert this into a drama worth reporting to their viewers and readers. Do they think after Stanley is dug up, he is going to walk down to where they are and answer questions?

Stanley is not the only one who won't be responding to media queries. I won't either, because I don't want to discuss what we are hoping or expecting to find. I don't want to have to eat my words if it turns out that Stanley died from eating too much bacon and desserts and not exercising.

Of course, it has been widely reported what is going on, and what today's purpose is. I just don't want to be quoted on it.

The only people within proximity of the "action" are Laurie and me, two people from Kathryn Strickland's office, and a crew that the coroner has sent. The crew are operating excavating equipment; then the coffin will be lifted out by machine in the same manner it was probably lowered in.

Laurie and I are here to keep everyone on their toes, but we really serve no function. They could be bringing Stanley's mother up and we wouldn't know the difference. And I sure as hell don't want to look into the coffin to confirm anything.

The whole process takes two and a half of the most boring hours I have ever spent. But what's left of Stanley is finally loaded onto the medical examiner's truck and driven away. I'm sure the media will get some photos and video of it as it passes by.

It's going to take two weeks to get the results; if the prosecution had requested it, it would probably take an hour and a half. We've hired experts to watch what they do, which is no doubt a waste of money. Laurie knows most of the people at the lab, and she has full confidence in their honesty. I'm a bit less trusting.

"That was fun," Laurie says as we leave. "You really know how to show a girl a good time."

"Stick with me, babe."

This was a great idea," I say.

Laurie smiles. "I just can't believe you went along with it."

I've been obsessing over the Wasserman case since I jumped in. Not only is it the only way I know how to do it, but it's required. A lawyer has to be on top of everything, the master of every detail, because a murder trial always presents twists and turns that must be anticipated and prepared for.

But with the trial starting tomorrow, I am ready. Not confident, but ready. So Laurie suggested we go out to dinner tonight, with the thought that it would help me relax.

She was right. We've gone to the Bonfire, on Market Street near Route 20, not far from our house. I've been coming here all my life and have continued even though it switched to Caribbean food a while back. I wouldn't want to eat this cuisine regularly, but once in a while I enjoy it, and I don't need to use chopsticks.

Ricky's coming home next week, so we talk about how great it will be to see him. And we talk about the Mets' dwindling chance to make the playoffs, and about the Giants' dim prospects in the upcoming football season.

We talk about a lot of other stuff as well, but one thing we don't talk about is the case. We are having dinner in a trial-free zone.

I even have a drink, one with a Spanish name I can't pronounce. It has vodka and all kinds of nectars and some kind of lychee fruit. I wouldn't know a lychee fruit if I found a tree of them growing in my living room, but it's delicious.

Laurie does not have one, which makes her the designated driver going home.

We spend ninety relaxing minutes having dinner. I know I'm going to go home and pore through the trial documents again later, but for now I am keeping them far from my mind.

I pay the check and we go outside. It's only eight o'clock, we're not exactly night owls, and there is some traffic on the street, heading toward the highway. Route 80 is also right nearby with easy access, and it's a quick fifteen-to-twenty-minute drive to the George Washington Bridge.

Laurie walks out first, with me just behind her. We head for our car, which is parked on the street. I see a car pull out of a parking spot in the direction we are going and drive toward us. I notice it because the car's lights are not on.

As it approaches, it slows down, and the driver's window starts to open. I am not the sharpest tool in the shed at times like this, and the only reason I realize something is wrong is when Laurie screams, "Andy!"

I see a glimmer of metal in the open window, and the hint of a driver's face behind it in the darkness. Suddenly a shot rings out; the sound is unmistakable.

Next there is the sound of glass shattering, but it doesn't seem to be the glass in the driver's window. There is a second shot, and then the car speeds up as it goes down the street. By now Laurie and I have gone to the ground, so I don't see the car crash off another parked car and then into a telephone pole, before coming to rest.

Laurie stands back up first, and I see that she is holding a handgun. A lot of yelling and screaming is coming from people in the area, but I can't understand what they are saying.

I finally stand up and see Marcus Clark, holding a gun of his own, running toward the crashed car. Laurie follows him, then I do. "Stay back, Andy," she says, as she and Marcus approach the car, guns drawn and ready to be fired.

She and Marcus finally reach the car and look into the window. Since nothing happens, I venture forward and look in.

Unfortunately, Laurie has taken out her phone and used its flashlight to shine into the car, so I get to see a truly disgusting sight, one that my stomach, filled with a Caribbean dinner, is going to have trouble dealing with.

A man is in the driver's seat, and while he still has a head, it is covered by a bloody mask. His mouth has a weird expression, almost a smile, but it can't be that he's pleased with the evening's events.

I know I'm not.

I have nothing to say; I'm afraid of what might happen if I open my mouth.

Laurie breaks the silence. "Nice shot, Marcus."

I didn't get to study the trial documents after dinner last night.

We were outside the restaurant until almost one in the morning as the police reconstructed everything that had happened. The whole thing took about twenty seconds; I'm not sure why it took five hours for us to recount it to the detective's satisfaction.

It would have been worse, but Pete Stanton was in charge of the scene. He is the captain of the Homicide Division of Paterson PD, and since the Bonfire is in Paterson, and he heard I was involved, he came down to supervise.

Marcus had been in the area watching out for me, as Laurie had insisted. He noticed a car parked about a hundred feet down the street from the restaurant. A man was in the car, and Marcus saw that the man spent the entire time staring at the restaurant entrance.

Marcus then moved closer to the restaurant, so that he was between the suspicious car and the entrance. He saw Laurie and me come out, and the car pulled out and moved toward us, making Marcus certain the man was up to no good. Marcus saw the window open, then the reflection off the gun barrel, so he fired off a round of his own.

Nice shot, Marcus.

The man, likely already dead, pressed the trigger on his

gun and the shot went up into the air, probably falling harm-lessly somewhere in Clifton. The glass that shattered was the passenger-side window; Marcus's shot had the staying power to go through the man's head and still crash through it.

The media descended on the scene. I refused all interviews, but Laurie did not. I had asked her to tell them the attempt was made to stop my investigation into the Tony Wasserman case. Because of the gag order implemented by Judge Lofton, I was prohibited from saying that, but Laurie was not.

Pete told me that the assailant's name on his identification was Christopher Marrero. He had a Michigan license with a De-troit address. I told Pete truthfully that I didn't know him.

Pete's answer was direct and to the point: "He knew you."

When Laurie and I got home, we sat in the den and had some wine. I love being home, with Laurie and the dogs, and it rarely felt better than last night.

I was secretly hoping to have post-drive-by-shooting-attempt sex. I mean, when am I going to get another chance? But I think we were both too shaken up. We were also exhausted and had no trouble falling asleep.

I'm not terribly in the mood to begin the trial this morning, but that would likely be true any morning. We are starting by holding a special meeting that the judge has called in his cham-bers. It's just the Judge, Strickland, and me; no court reporter is present.

Strickland is already here when I arrive, and she stands. "Andy, I'm glad you're okay."

"Thanks."

"As am I," Judge Lofton says, and I thank him as well.

We sit down, and the judge asks whether either of us thinks this should impact or delay the trial.

Strickland speaks first. "Your Honor, we have no need for a delay, but if Mr. Carpenter needs or wants one, we would have no objection. What we want to avoid, though, is a direct connection being made between the incident last night and this case. To my knowledge, no such link has been established."

"It will be," I say.

I'm torn here; my preference would be to delay the trial until the Mets win a World Series or the world comes to an end, whichever comes first. But I spoke to Tony, and he strongly wants to move forward as quickly as possible.

"We don't seek a delay either, Judge. But I appreciate your making the offer."

"Very well. Let's get to it."

Kathryn Strickland controls a courtroom.

I thought that was true during the earlier hearing, when the place was mostly empty. Now, with a packed gallery, a significant media presence, and a filled jury box, it's even more obvious.

She stands to give her opening statement, but pauses before she begins, as if collecting her thoughts. Every person in the entire room, with the exception of me, is anxious to hear what she has to say.

She starts with a smile. "You are the chosen twelve. Some of you are no doubt pleased by that, and I suspect that some of you are not. It can be a physical hardship, having to come here every day. It can be an economic hardship; some of you are probably missing work to be here, or perhaps having to hire child care to make up for your absence.

"It can be a mental hardship, because you must concentrate intently on every word spoken. And it can be an emotional hardship, because a man's life is in your hands, and you are seeking justice for a life already lost.

"So on behalf of the State of New Jersey, and the people of Bergen County, I thank you for your service. If it's any consolation, I can tell you that at the end of the day it's all worth it, because what you are doing is incredibly important.

"You are here to decide whether or not Anthony Wasserman, with premeditation, committed the homicide of Rachel Wasserman Morehouse. Ms. Morehouse had been married to Stanley Wasserman, which made Anthony Wasserman her stepson.

"You will hear that Anthony Wasserman, the defendant, had a strained relationship with his father, Stanley, and virtually no relationship with his stepmother, Rachel.

"If you do not know it already, you will learn that Stanley Wasserman was incredibly, almost incomprehensibly wealthy, and that his wealth was transferred to Rachel Morehouse when he passed.

"You will learn that Anthony Wasserman stood to get three hundred thousand dollars when both of his parents passed. Now that may seem like a lot of money, and it is, but let me give you an example of how wealthy the Wassermans were, and why Anthony was so upset to be getting what he was getting.

"Had Anthony Wasserman received ten million dollars, it would have represented point zero zero zero eight of the entire estate. To get just one percent of the estate, he would have had to receive one hundred and twenty million dollars. And the three hundred thousand that was left to Anthony? That represented point zero zero zero zero two five percent of the estate. That's right . . . four zeros before you even get to a number.

"So he was upset, and you know what? I might have been upset also. The difference is that I would not have responded by committing murder.

"The evidence will show that Rachel Morehouse was killed by an injection of potassium chloride, which caused her heart to stop. That drug was uniquely dangerous to her because of an existing heart condition, so someone with knowledge of her condition would logically have picked it.

"Anthony Wasserman lived with Rachel Morehouse for the

three weeks before she died, so he was in position to have that knowledge. He is also a chemist, so he had the expertise required to prepare the drug. And traces of the drug were found in his car and room, and he argued vehemently with Rachel the morning she died.

"You will hear all of this from witnesses in a position to know, and then you will make the judgment as to whether Anthony Wasserman murdered Rachel Wasserman Morehouse, beyond a reasonable doubt.

"Now I must tell you, all the evidence presented to you will be what we call circumstantial. All that means is that no one was an eyewitness to the crime; no one actually saw it take place.

"But if an eyewitness account were necessary, how many murderers would go free? Because most want to do their act in private, so as not to be caught. So, yes, this evidence is circumstantial, but it is powerful and irrefutable.

"You will get to hear the evidence, all of the evidence, and you will make a collective decision. I am confident that it will be the correct one."

I decide to give my opening now, rather than exercise my right to wait for the start of the defense case. Judge Lofton sends everyone to lunch first, which is fine with me. I do not want to talk to jurors wondering when and what they are going to get to eat. Besides, most of the jurors are still counting the zeros that Strickland spoke about in her opening.

I'm at lunch when Corey Douglas shows up to give me the bad news. The lab tests are back and conclusive; Samuel Wasserman was not murdered. No traces of drugs of any kind were in his remains. It's disappointing; it would have helped our case if he was murdered while Tony was teaching high school chemistry in Indiana.

Laurie has also found out that we will not get to exhume the body of Arnold Etheridge, the Minneapolis executive who ran a Wasserman company and was said to have died of a heart attack. Mr. Etheridge had been cremated.

After lunch I get up to give my opening, but I first look at Tony, who sits between Eddie Dowd and me at the defense table. I've told him to look impassive and remain expressionless throughout the trial, but I can see he's struggling with it. It couldn't have been easy this morning to hear someone eloquently say that you should spend the rest of your life in jail.

"Ladies and gentlemen, I agree with a lot of what Ms. Strickland said this morning." I smile. "Well, mostly the early stuff. She said it better than I could, so I'll just associate myself with her remarks. Your job is difficult, and crucial, and I thank you for doing it.

"One thing she didn't mention is the pressure that you are under, but there is a ton of pressure and it will be intense. Because there is no way to sugarcoat this: You have a decision to make, a judgment to render, and you know what? You'd better get it right.

"It will come as no surprise to you that there are many things Ms. Strickland said that I disagree with. That's the nature of the process, and you will hear those disagreements very clearly as the trial moves on. We will be saying very different things, and it will be up to you to decide who is right.

"But for now I'd like to focus on what Ms. Strickland did not say. These are important points . . . and there are quite a few of them.

"For example, she didn't tell you that Tony Wasserman is a high school teacher from Indiana who put himself through college and never asked his father for a thing. She didn't tell you that Tony has never been convicted of a crime, never charged, never arrested, never accused. He has not committed a violent act in his entire life, yet suddenly, at the age of forty-three, he becomes a premeditated murderer?

"Ms. Strickland told you that as a chemist Tony knew how to make this drug, but she didn't tell you that anyone can buy it at a pharmacy. She would have you believe that he took the most difficult path and produced it himself and then went sprinkling it all over his car and room, so the police could find it. Does that make sense?

"She didn't tell you that Rachel Morehouse was ill with cancer and heart disease, yet spent her final days trying to effect huge changes at the company she inherited. Because that company, as Rachel learned, was a criminal enterprise and was responsible for a number of murders to protect their operation.

"Rachel Wasserman Morehouse became their latest, and hopefully last, victim.

"But one of the best things about our system is that you should not take my word for any of this, or for that matter, Ms. Strickland's. Because what we say is argument, not evidence.

"You will listen to the witnesses and hear the facts, and here is another place where I agree with Ms. Strickland. I too am confident you will make the correct decision.

"Thank you."

J udge Lofton adjourns court, telling the jury, lawyers, and everyone else in listening distance that we will start with witnesses tomorrow.

As I head toward the rear doors, I see that Laurie is waiting for me.

"You have the look of someone who has learned something."

She nods. "I put the time you were giving your speech to good use."

Laurie had dropped me off at the courthouse this morning; she was going down to the precinct to learn whatever she could from Pete.

"Christopher Marrero had no police record of any kind, was never charged with anything. He had residences in Detroit and Houston and lived in each place for two weeks at a time. He listed his occupation as truck driver."

"Is that what he was?"

"No, at least not as far as anyone can tell. The trucking company he claimed to be his employer was fake, which is a pretty good sign that he was not what he appeared."

"I would say so. Anything else?"

"Not yet, but Pete said he would keep us informed."

I don't know what to make of this. I have no doubt that Marrero's attempt on my life was tied into this case, but I don't know why they would risk such a public way of doing it. And as far as I know, Wasserman Equities does not own any companies in Detroit or Houston, so it's unclear where Marrero fits in.

But according to Pete, Marrero was either a pro or wildly overconfident in his abilities. For him to think he could make an accurate shot while driving in a car shows that this was not his first rodeo.

Of course, the fact that Marcus Clark was able to fire a perfect shot into that same moving car shows that it can be done, but there is only one Marcus Clark.

We order a pizza in for dinner, and when it arrives, Laurie goes to the door to pay for it. It's a fairly blatant way to keep me out of harm's way, just in case the pizza guy has a gun to go with the pepperoni topping. It turns out that he doesn't; all he brought was the pizza.

At around eight thirty, Pete Stanton calls and asks if he can come over. This must be something significant because there is a Mets game tonight and Pete is not at Charlie's watching it.

"You didn't go to Charlie's?" I ask when Pete comes over.

"No. I've found that I need to go at least one night a week without seeing pictures of Vince's dog."

"It is irritating."

"And he must hug that stupid dog all the time; he's always got dog hair all over him. He looks like Grizzly Adams. The other night I found a dog hair in my beer; they must be flying off of him."

"You should stop going there," Laurie says.

He looks at her like she's nuts. "And start paying for my own food?"

"Sorry, Laurie doesn't know just how cheap you are. If you're finished venting about Vince and his dog, any more on Marrero?"

"Yes, but more means less in this case."

"That's a little cryptic, Pete," Laurie says.

"Everything about him is fake. They've examined documents he's filled out, applications for credit cards, bank accounts . . . stuff like that. The guy is made up, nothing about him is real. It's the most professional fake identity any of our people have ever seen."

"Where did he get money to live on?"

"That's the only thing about him that's real; he had plenty of money. It was wired to him every month from an untraceable account. No way to tell from who or what he did to earn it."

"I think we have an idea," Laurie says. "He was a hit man, on retainer."

"This goes way beyond that," Pete says.

I am about to ask Pete to do something, and then I realize Sam can probably do it better, and certainly faster.

"So he had credit cards in the name Chris Marrero?"

"Absolutely. And bank accounts, and rental leases, and a car, all in that name. That's been his life for quite more than seven years. But before that, nothing."

"This is not good," Laurie says. "Somebody with the resources to employ Marrero that way would be sure to have other options."

Pete turns to me. "She's right. Make sure Marcus stays nearby. I don't want to have to buy my own beer."

As soon as he leaves, even before Laurie can start lecturing me on how careful I need to be, I call Sam.

"I've got another assignment for you and your team, Sam."

"Talk to me."

"You need to do a deep dive on Christopher Marrero, the guy who Marcus nailed. He was from Detroit, or at least he had a house and car there."

"How deep?"

"Total. I especially want to know his travel records, and whether any correspond to the deaths at the Wasserman companies. If he was in any of those areas around the same time, that would be crucial."

"And you need it immediately?"

"Even faster."

"We're pretty backed up, Andy. You okay if I bring in more help?"

"Sure. Who do you have in mind?"

"Irv Feldman. He lives in the same building as the Mandlebaums. I've never met him, but Hilda says he's even better on a computer than she is. She says he can hack into anything; he hasn't paid a phone or electric bill in three years."

"How old is he?"

"Eighty-nine, but Hilda says eighty-nine is the new eighty-four."

"Sam, you better hurry up and hire Irv before someone else grabs him."

I am not surprised that Bernie Hudson is Strickland's first witness.

Even though the prosecution does not have to prove or even demonstrate motive, juries always look for it. Jurors are instructed to be logical, and that brings with it the implicit need to find the reason for the crime.

Put simply, it makes it easier for them to decide the defendant committed the crime if they can figure out why.

The why, according to the entire prosecution case, is money. It's the money that Stanley Wasserman had, and that Rachel Morehouse inherited. It's also the money that they claim Tony Wasserman coveted.

Strickland is painstaking in her approach; we could be in for a long trial. She takes fifteen minutes to take Bernie through his career path, building up his bona fides as a top attorney. I don't think it is necessary; Bernie is a lawyer, the executor of Rachel's will, and strictly a fact witness.

"You prepared Rachel Morehouse's will?" Strickland finally gets around to asking.

"I did. At her direction."

"So you were her attorney and the executor of the will?"

"Yes."

"Is that unusual?"

"It frequently happens that way. If a person has a relationship with their attorney and trusts them, that person often sees that attorney as a logical person to be the executor."

"Did you serve in that role for Stanley Wasserman as well?"

"I did not."

"What was the approximate value of Rachel Morehouse's estate at the time of her death?"

"Twelve point two billion dollars."

"That's billion with a *b*?"

"That's the only way I know how to spell it."

"How much of that money was directed to go to Anthony Wasserman?"

"Three hundred thousand dollars."

"Did that strike you as a small amount?"

Bernie shakes his head. "It's not my role to make judgments about things like this. I execute my client's wishes."

"Did your client ever discuss with you why she chose that amount?"

Bernie looks uncomfortable. The judge has given him a waiver on privilege issues, so he is free to discuss communications with Rachel. But it obviously still goes against his grain and training.

"She did not. But it was the money that Stanley Wasserman directed her to leave."

"Was she free to change that and leave him more or less if she so chose?"

He nods. "Yes, she was."

"Did she have plans to amend the will, if you know?" Strickland is bringing this up in her direct examination, rather than let me do it, because it cuts slightly more in the defense's favor.

"She did. We had a meeting planned, but she passed away before that meeting could take place."

"Was the will a complex document, relatively speaking?"

"Very."

"And the amending she planned could have been about any of many different things?"

"Certainly."

"Did she indicate that it related to Mr. Wasserman?"

"She did, in part. I had the feeling that it was about other things as well."

There is not much for me to do on cross-examination, and certainly not in the area of what the will contained. Bernie just gave the facts, which I obviously can't challenge. The area for me to home in on was the planned amendment to the will.

"Mr. Hudson, did Rachel Morehouse ever express a dislike for Tony Wasserman?"

"No. I think the one time she spoke of him to me, and it must have been a year ago, she said that they never had much of a relationship. She said someday she hoped to change that."

"So she wanted to be closer to him?"

"I've really said all that I remember about the conversation."

"Are you aware that Mr. Wasserman had spent a few weeks at Mrs. Morehouse's house before her death?"

"Yes."

"And it was during that time that she said she wanted to meet to amend her will?"

"Yes."

"How long had it been since she had previously amended it, if ever?"

"About a year and a half ago."

"And she could have been planning to leave Mr. Wasserman far more money, you just don't know either way?"

"That is correct."

"Thank you, no further questions."

Strickland establishes on redirect that she could also have been planning to cut Tony out of the three hundred grand. "Would you say that's a lot of money for a person on a teacher's salary?"

"I suppose it is."

But my point has been made, and the first witness is behind us.

We're off and running.

New Jersey is not exactly careful about how they spend my tax dollars.

They have gone to the expense of flying in a witness from Indiana and putting him up in a hotel, all to get him to say something of little consequence on the witness stand. On behalf of my fellow citizens, I hope they flew him coach.

The witness is Terry Capria, a colleague of Tony's at the high school where he teaches. Capria is a science teacher and has been a friend of Tony's for the last five years.

Strickland takes some time to establish that relationship, then gets to the crux of the matter. I know what he is going to say because I saw the transcript of the interview he did with the police.

"Did Mr. Wasserman ever talk about his father?"

"He did. Once."

"What were the circumstances?"

"I actually read a newspaper story about his father's death. I think it was in *The New York Times*; I subscribe online."

"So it was an obituary?"

"My recollection is that it was more than that, more like a news story."

"Go on. . . ."

"It mentioned that he was survived by his son, Anthony, of

Evansville, Indiana. I never knew or thought Tony came from a wealthy family, so I asked if the story was referring to him. He said that it was."

"What did you say?"

"Well, first I said I was sorry for his loss, but he didn't seem too upset. Once he made that clear, I made a joke . . . something like 'Does this mean we're rich?'"

"What did Mr. Wasserman say?"

"He said, 'The next dime I get from that son of a bitch will be the first.'"

"You remember that clearly?"

"I do. It surprised me when he said it. Anyway, I backed off after that and didn't mention his father again. And I don't think he ever did either, at least not to me."

Strickland turns the witness over to me.

"Mr. Capria, you consider Mr. Wasserman a friend, correct?"

"Definitely. I hope my appearance here doesn't do anything to change that."

"So you want to remain his friend?"

"Of course."

"Do you befriend a great many murderers?"

"Of course not."

"Does that mean you don't believe Tony Wasserman murdered anyone?"

"I do not believe it." Capria says it with authority, just the way I would have told him to had I gotten a chance to prepare him.

"Have you ever known him to be violent?"

"Never."

"You wouldn't be at all nervous to be around him if he was angry at you?"

"Absolutely not."

"You'd be comfortable having your family around him?"

"Of course. We've all been together many times."

"Have you ever referred to someone as a son of a bitch?"

"I'm afraid I have. Quite a few times."

"Did you ever kill any of those people?"

"Of course not."

"Thank you."

Brooke Schlosser is an important witness for the prosecution.

She is the only person that can testify about anger between Tony and Rachel; she says she heard them arguing the morning of Rachel's death. It is significant testimony if I can't challenge it.

"You're a neighbor of Ms. Morehouse?" Strickland asks.

"Yes. I live fairly close."

With her insatiable need for overkill, Strickland introduces a large map of the area as evidence. She shows where the two houses are, unnecessarily confirming that they are neighbors.

Strickland gets Schlosser to say that she was taking her dog for a walk past Rachel's house and, as usual, stopped to see if Rachel wanted to join her with Lion.

"Did she do that often?"

Schlosser nods. "Oh, yes. Lion loved to go for walks, so Rachel took him whenever she could. When she wasn't feeling great, I often took both dogs."

"Did you have occasion to meet the defendant?"

Schlosser nods, glancing at Tony. "Yes, on two occasions, maybe three. Once we even all had lunch together."

"So you spoke to him? You heard his voice?"

"Of course."

"Tell us what happened on the morning of the day Rachel

Morehouse died when you approached the house with your dog."

"I heard Rachel and Tony . . . the defendant . . . arguing. They were loud and sounded angry."

"Could you hear what they were saying?"

"Not really. They were yelling over each other, so it was hard to make out."

"But you're sure the voice you heard was Mr. Wasserman?"

"I'm certain of it, yes."

"Thank you."

I liked Brooke Schlosser when I met her, mainly because I liked how she treated her golden retriever. Unfortunately, I am going to have to take her apart.

"Ms. Schlosser, when you approached the house, did you see a car in the driveway?"

"Yes."

"Did that surprise you?"

"I didn't think much about it at the time, but it was unusual for a car to be there. Rachel and Mr. Wasserman would park in the garage."

"What kind of car was it?"

"I have no idea. I'm not good with cars, and I had no reason to remember."

"Color?"

"I don't know. I think it was dark."

I introduce as evidence a copy of the police forensics report that describes Tony's car. I have Schlosser read the color: "White."

"So it could have been someone else's car?'

"It's possible; I really wouldn't know."

"Those times you met Mr. Wasserman, including during the lunch, you learned what his voice sounded like?"

"I didn't learn it, but I heard it enough to recognize it."

"Did he yell a lot during those meetings?"

"No."

"Was he angry at you?"

"No."

"So his tone was different than what you heard that morning?"

"Oh, yes. This was a very angry voice."

"But you could still recognize it?"

"Oh, yes."

I introduce as evidence a digital recording I made. "There are three different male voices yelling on this tape. I am going to play it, and I'd like you to tell me which one is Mr. Wasserman."

I see Strickland wanting to object and trying to come up with a rationale to do so. She can't find one because there isn't one that would be successful. I have a right to do this to test the witness's credibility.

Schlosser looks a bit nervous about all this, but all she can do is listen as I play the recording. One after another, the three men yell, "You're wrong! You can't do that! I won't let you!"

When I'm finished, she says, "Can I hear it again?"

"Of course," I say, ever agreeable. So I play it again. All this time the courtroom is otherwise completely silent.

"It's the third one," she says with some relief that she has recognized it. "The third person yelling is Mr. Wasserman."

"Are you certain of that?"

She nods. "I'm pretty sure, yes."

I introduce a video, which I say will be self-explanatory. When it's projected, it is the video version of the audiotape, in that we can see the three men who were yelling. None of them are Tony Wasserman.

Next I introduce a notarized deposition from Richard McCauley, professor of linguistics at Rutgers. He supervised the whole thing and can be seen in the video. He attests that it's all real and not doctored.

"Just for the record," I say, "the voice you identified belonged to Dan Dowling, my veterinarian. He is not a suspect in this case; he has an alibi. He was neutering a cat that morning."

Before Strickland can object, Judge Lofton admonishes me to not make a mockery of the courtroom. I promise to behave.

"Ms. Schlosser, is it possible you were wrong about the voice you heard?"

"I suppose so, but I still think I was right."

"Which time are you referring to when you say you were right? The day in the driveway when things were so muffled you couldn't make out the words, or just now, when everything was crystal clear?"

"In the driveway."

I frown my feigned disappointment at her not admitting her error and thank her for her time. She's upset; when she gets home, her golden can console her.

They're great at that.

W e're going to have to start presenting the defense case next week. The only way we can do that is to figure out what is going on at the Wasserman companies that has resulted in these deaths.

A vague idea is brewing in my head, but it's all based on suppositions and guesswork. Juries do not respond well to suppositions and guesswork, but that doesn't matter, because Judge Lofton would never let them hear it in the first place.

I assemble the team for a quick meeting to give out assignments. "We have to move, and move quickly. That may mean we waste some time and effort, but if we're lucky, it also could pay off." I have two big jobs to assign. "Corey, I need you to go to Philadelphia. Actually, King of Prussia."

"What for?"

"Callan, the guy who died from the peanut allergy, ran Winston Pharmaceutical. They have a factory in King of Prussia, and I want you to keep an eye on it."

"What am I looking for?"

"Trucks belonging to National Trucking. That's the Minneapolis company that Arnold Etheridge sold to Wasserman, and shortly after that he had the sudden heart attack."

"And if I see any?"

"That's enough for now. But they may show up after hours,

well into the night. I spoke to Willie Miller, and he'll go with you, so that you can cover the place all day. If one goes in, I want to know how long it takes before it leaves again."

"You think they're manufacturing drugs to sell on the street?"

"It wouldn't surprise me."

I turn to my cyber expert. "And, Sam, I have something else for you. I want you to do a deep dive on the headhunter firm that Wasserman owned."

"That's the one where the CEO was killed in the hit-and-run."

"Right. I want to know if there are any industries they specialize in. I need a list of everyone they have placed in jobs in the past three years."

"That will be a long list."

"I doubt it will be as long as you think, but we can whittle it down after I see it. I also want to know if the number of clients that they placed in jobs increased or decreased after the new management came in. Can you get into their system?"

"Of course."

"Good. Any luck on Global Aviation flights coming in from Portugal?"

"No, nothing yet."

"Have you brought in Irv Feldman?"

"I have; he's as good as Hilda said, maybe even better."

"Great. Let's work his eighty-nine-year-old ass into the ground."

Susan Wolford is next up on Strickland's greatest-hits list. She is important because she is the one witness who can talk of discord between Rachel and Tony.

"Ms. Wolford, how did you come to know Rachel More-house?"

"You mean originally?" The question annoys me, first because Strickland obviously meant originally, and second because Wolford knows exactly what she means. The prosecution no doubt prepped Wolford intensively for this appearance; nothing that is asked will come as a surprise or actually be confusing to Wolford.

"Yes, originally."

"Well, my husband, Jim, worked for Stanley Wasserman at Wasserman Equities. They also had a friendship outside of work. Years after Stanley's divorce, he met Rachel, so I first knew her then. We would go out to dinner occasionally, the four of us, and then of course there were business functions."

"So you knew her even before she and Stanley were married?"

"Yes, but then obviously after they married, we spent even more time together."

"You considered Rachel a good friend?"

"Very good."

"Did you know the defendant, Anthony Wasserman?"

"Certainly not well. We met a couple of times while he was staying with Rachel in the weeks before she died."

"Did she talk about him with you?" Strickland asks.

"Yes. Actually we spoke about him on that same morning."

"You were at her house?"

Wolford nods. "Yes, for coffee. We did that quite often."

"What did she say about Mr. Wasserman?"

"She said that things were not working out. She was sad about it."

"Did she say why?"

"Yes, although Rachel didn't speak much about personal things. She said that there was just too much baggage, that the family issues ran deep."

"Was Mr. Wasserman in the house while you spoke?"

"I believe he was, yes. Rachel whispered when she talked about him, she said she didn't want him to overhear us."

"Thank you. No further questions."

"Ms. Wolford, did Rachel express any fear of Tony?" is how I start my cross.

"Not to me."

"Did she say she wanted him out of the house, or that she was going to call the police for protection? Anything like that?"

"No."

"Did you and Rachel ever talk about Wasserman Equities?"

"Not a lot. That was Jim's . . . that's my husband . . . his area. My friendship with Rachel was strictly personal."

"Did you know that it was her plan, and she actually started executing it, to become more involved in the business? To take an active role in running it?"

"I knew she was becoming more involved, yes. Jim was happy about that."

"Did you know that she was concerned about irregularities in the business, and that she was intent on ending them?"

"No, I—"

Strickland objects that this is outside the scope of proper cross-examination because it wasn't discussed on direct. She's right, and Judge Lofton sustains her objection. I'm fine with that; I simply wanted to get the jury to hear the question, so that they can tie it into my case later on.

I let Wolford off the stand. I did not accomplish much, but there was no opportunity for me to do so. Hopefully better days are ahead.

Once I leave the courtroom, I turn on my cell phone and see a message from Corey to call him; he had called this morning. I call him back right away.

"What have you got?"

"One of the National trucks came into Winston Pharmaceutical at nine o'clock last night, long after the regular shift had gone home. It left more than three hours later, at twelve thirty A.M."

"Good."

"I know you didn't tell us to, but Willie and I followed it, at least to its first stop."

"Where was it?"

"A rest area, just off the Pennsylvania Turnpike. There was another truck waiting for it there. We obviously had to stay at a distance, so we couldn't see exactly what was going on, but they were definitely transferring material from the National truck to the one that was waiting."

"Were there any markings on the other truck?"

"None that we could see, but it was dark, and even though we had binoculars, we were pretty far away."

"What's your best guess?" I already know the answer. It's the answer I wanted, so I just want to hear him say it.

"A truck that apparently just made a pickup at a pharmaceutical manufacturing company drops off merchandise at midnight at a rest stop. Gee, I can't imagine what it might be."

"We need to get the DEA involved. I have a connection—"

"So do I," says Corey. "Gary Kimbrell. He works out of the Trenton office; he'll eat this up with a spoon."

"Good, then set it up. Next time this truck makes a run, we want to make sure their first stop is an interesting one."

Sergeant Kurt Bennett has been in the forensics department of the Bergen County Sheriff's Office for years.

I've never met him or had reason to encounter him on the stand because most of my cases have been in Passaic County. But I've asked around about him, and by all accounts he is competent, a straight shooter, and an excellent witness.

He's certainly never worked on an easier case than this one. There was essentially no murder scene known for at least two weeks because it took that long for it to be considered a murder.

But even though Bennett had little to do, he has emerged as one of the two key prosecution witnesses. And the one thing he has in common with his fellow witnesses is that there is little I can do to challenge him.

I am in the uncomfortable position of being unable to dismantle the prosecution's case, leaving me no choice but to create an entirely alternate version that the jury can find credible enough to cause reasonable doubt.

Strickland asks questions that allow Bennett to talk about his career in forensics, his case experience, and his expertise. He comes across well, forthright and a bit humble. Definitely the kind of guy that jurors will believe does not have an ax to grind.

"Were you in charge of the forensics investigation on this case?" Strickland finally asks.

"I was. I am."

"Please describe your involvement."

"Well, at first there was none. Ms. Morehouse appeared to be a heart attack victim, likely of natural causes. So there was no murder scene to speak of because no one realized there was a murder at all."

"When did you get called in?"

"After the autopsy. I was told to look for traces of potassium chloride, which I did, after the detectives secured a search warrant."

"Did you find any?"

"Yes. In the bedroom that was used by Mr. Wasserman and in the trunk of his car."

I'm actually surprised that Strickland did not have the coroner testify before Bennett. Once the coroner had established that potassium chloride was the agent that caused the death, Bennett's talk of finding it would have more significance. But it will all come out in the end anyway.

Strickland turns the witness over to me, and once again I approach with few bullets in my gun.

"Sergeant, when you went to Rachel Morehouse's home, did you walk through other rooms besides Anthony Wasserman's?"

"Yes, his room was in the back of the house."

"Did you find the other rooms to be clean?"

He smiles. "Spotless. I talked to the housekeeper, who mentioned that she cleaned every day, even after Ms. Morehouse died. She said it kept her busy."

"Was Mr. Wasserman's room similarly clean?"

"No, it wasn't."

"Did you ask the housekeeper why that was?"

"I did. She said Mr. Wasserman told her it wasn't necessary, that he would clean it himself."

"And did he? As best as you can tell?"

"Not really, no."

"Had he cleaned his room, or had the housekeeper cleaned it like she did the rest of the house, would you have found trace levels of potassium chloride? After two weeks of cleaning?"

"No way to know for sure, but it's unlikely."

"So it's fair to say that the defendant could likely have removed the evidence that you found in his room, but chose not to?"

"Probably fair . . . yes. Of course I don't know why he made that choice."

"I understand. And while we're discussing things you don't know, do you know how the potassium chloride got in the places you found it?"

"No."

"You don't know if Mr. Wasserman put it there?"

"No."

"You don't know if someone else put it there, to implicate Mr. Wasserman?"

"No."

"Thank you."

On the way home, Sam calls and says he has an update on the headhunting firm, so I go down to his office instead. It also gives me a chance to meet Irv Feldman and to have some pre-dinner, appetite-spoiling rugelach.

Sam gives me a list of people the company has placed in jobs the last three years. "You're right," he says. "It's smaller than I thought, and much less than before Wasserman took over."

"You have the industries they specialize in?"

"It's in the envelope with the list of names."

I had hoped to watch a Mets game tonight, but instead I'm going to be poring over this list. It's just as well; they're playing the Dodgers and Kershaw is pitching. Ricky's team had a better chance of beating Clifton.

The prosecution case is nearing its end, which only increases the pressure on us to come up with something.

Tomorrow is Friday, and my belief is that Strickland will drag her case out until the end of the day, so that we don't begin ours until Monday. That will give the jury the entire weekend to think about how guilty Tony is.

I take the dogs for a walk, hoping for some inspiration, divine or otherwise. But all I come back with is an almost-filled plastic bag, mostly courtesy of Sebastian. The symbolism is not lost on me . . . we are in deep shit.

During dinner with Laurie, we decide that she will go to the bus stop Saturday to pick up Ricky without me. It pains me to do it this way, but I need to spend every minute working on the case. Ricky will understand, probably helped by some future therapist that he's been driven to by an uncaring, absent father.

Sam calls with some significant news. "There's a Global Aviation flight to Newark arriving Tuesday night. Same time as always, due in at ten fifteen."

Since today is Thursday, that gives us plenty of time to prepare. "Excellent. When people in that area use one of Global's planes for domestic travel, do they use a private airport?"

"Probably, but I'd have to confirm."

"Okay. If they do, I need to know which airport they use.

I would think Global has deals with private airports, so there probably would be only one in that location that they always take off and land from."

"I'll get back to you."

Five minutes later Sam does.

"What took you so long?"

Sam doesn't consider that worthy of a reply. "They use Masterson Aviation as their private airport."

"And that's the only one in the area?"

"It is."

"Perfect."

I ask Sam to do something else for me, to drive down there and take as many pictures of the place as he can. I want to know where the planes land, and where they let off their passengers.

"I'm on it," he says.

Once I'm off the phone, I say to Laurie, "We're going to need Marcus."

"What for?"

"Unfortunately, he and I are going to spend Tuesday night together."

This is basically a science-driven prosecution case, and the key player to drive it home is the medical examiner for Bergen County, Maxine Auger.

She's had the job for twenty-two years and was the assistant medical examiner for seven years before that. So it's fair to say that testifying in this trial is not going to cause her sleepless nights and tremendous anxiety.

After establishing her credentials, Strickland asked her if they always perform autopsies when someone dies.

Auger shakes her head. "No, not if it appears that the person died of natural causes, especially if they were older or sick. Usually the deceased's doctor will confirm that, and an autopsy is not considered necessary."

"Was Rachel Morehouse's doctor consulted in this case?"

"Yes, and he said that Ms. Morehouse was suffering from cancer and heart disease."

"Which would ordinarily have caused you not to do the autopsy?"

"Correct."

"But you did perform one. What changed your mind?"

"My assistant, who went to the scene, noticed some unusual bruise marks on the wrists of the deceased, which would not be consistent with a fall. He also saw what he thought was a needle puncture wound in her vein on her left arm. He put that in his report, and when I saw that, I conducted my own examination to confirm his findings."

"And you did confirm them?"

"Yes. And it was unusual enough for me to decide an autopsy was necessary."

Strickland takes her through the scientific findings, that the death was caused by the potassium chloride. Auger describes how it would almost instantly have stopped Rachel's already weakened heart from beating.

On that note, Strickland turns the witness over to me.

"Doctor, if you know, can potassium chloride be purchased?"

"Yes, it can."

"It does not have to be mixed and created by a chemist?"

"That's correct."

"Can it be ingested orally?"

"Yes."

"The amount of potassium chloride in Rachel Morehouse's body, that would fit in one syringe?"

"Yes."

"Could it be hidden, perhaps in a bowl of soup or a cup of coffee?"

"I don't see why not."

"So if one were going to kill Rachel Morehouse, and one were living in her house for three weeks, there might have been an easier way to get her to receive the potassium chloride than holding her down and injecting it into her vein?"

Strickland objects that it calls for speculation, but Judge Lofton overrules, and Auger says, "I suppose so."

"Dr. Auger, you know for a scientific fact that Rachel Morehouse died of heart failure, caused by injection of potassium chloride into her arm. Is that correct?"

"Yes."

"Do you know for a fact, scientific or otherwise, who injected her?"

"I do not."

"Thank you."

Once Auger is off the stand, Strickland rises and says, with confidence, "Your Honor, the prosecution rests."

Our turn.

Uh-oh.

Today I wish I was a charter member of Sam's Bubeleh Brigade. It's Saturday, which is the Sabbath, which means they take the day off. No work, just relaxation, although hopefully Hilda considers baking to be relaxation. In any event, a day of no work sounds pretty good about now, since I'm going to be stuck poring over case documents all day.

At two o'clock, as Laurie is heading off to meet Ricky's bus, I decide that I need to go with her. It's more important for me to be there than it is to read the case documents for the twentieth time. I know them cold; going through them again is not going to help me any.

Watching Ricky come off that bus is going to help me a lot.

The prevailing view among the other parents waiting seems to be that, while they are anxious to see their kids, they could have handled another two weeks of relative freedom from responsibility.

Laurie and I don't share that view, and few sights are better than Ricky getting off that bus, lighting up when he sees us, and running to us for his first postcamp hugs.

All the way home he regales us with stories of his team's color-war victories, in which he seems to have played a major role. The only down moment is when he asks how the Mets have been doing, since he has little access to national sports news at camp. I have to break the bad news that the Mets won't be going to any playoff games unless they buy tickets.

Once we get home, Ricky joins me on a dog walk through East-side Park. We talk about the upcoming school year, prospects for the Giants season, and more about how much he loved camp. It's a pleasant walk, until he asks a question as we near the house.

"How's work, Dad?"

Well, I'm miserable, someone tried to kill me, and my innocent client may spend the rest of his life in jail is what I'm thinking but don't say. "Good, Rick, thanks for asking."

Marcus comes over at 7:00 P.M. to go over the plans for Tuesday night at the Masterson Airport. Laurie sits in as an interpreter; not only do I not understand a single word that Marcus says, but he is so outwardly unresponsive that I can never tell if he understands me.

But Marcus is extraordinarily smart, so I'm sure he understands exactly what is happening at all times. I just feel better if Laurie, as the Marcus whisperer, confirms it for me.

"Think of this as a reconnaissance mission," I say. "We're just trying to learn if I am right about what they are doing. There is no reason for us to try and intervene at this point; we want to be sure before we go that route."

Marcus doesn't say anything, of course, but I'm getting the vibe that he isn't thrilled with what he is hearing. Marcus likes to take action, but the truth is that he will only be there to protect me if I am somehow discovered.

"It's important that they don't see us. If they think we know what is going on, they might stop their operations for a while. We can't have that; when we make our move, it has to be at a time when I can still get it in front of the jury."

No answer from Marcus.

"We clear?"

"Yuhhh."

Obviously we're clear.

'm just getting into bed when Corey Douglas calls. It's only ten o'clock, but I wanted to make sure I got a good night's sleep so I can be fresh for court tomorrow.

"The truck just pulled in to Winston Pharmaceutical."

"Excellent," I say, because it is. "Is everything in place?"

"Willie and I are here, and Marcus is on the way. I've alerted my DEA friend and they are standing by, waiting for the go-ahead to go in."

The plan remains for Corey, Marcus, and Willie to alert the DEA agents when the truck leaves. The anticipation is that, like last time, that will happen in a few hours.

The expectation, and certainly the hope, is that the first stop the truck makes after it leaves will be at the same rest stop along the Pennsylvania Turnpike. But the DEA will be flexible and ready to adjust if that turns out not to be the case.

The early-sleep concept for tonight just went out the window. There is no way I am going to be able to sleep while waiting to hear what has happened. Besides, Corey has promised to update me as things take place, so the phone is going to keep ringing anyway.

Ricky is asleep, so Laurie and I plant ourselves in the den with glasses of wine to wait . . . and wait.

The truck pulled out of Winston Pharmaceutical at 12:15 A.M. Corey and Simon Garfunkel followed in Corey's car, while Marcus and Willie brought up the rear in Marcus's car.

Marcus and Willie lagged well behind, so the procession would not look like the Rose Bowl Parade. But Corey didn't have to get too close either; the truck wasn't traveling at a high speed, so there was no danger of losing it. Corey's assumption was that the truck wouldn't dare speed since it wouldn't want to get stopped by cops, not with the cargo it was carrying.

All went as planned. The truck did make the stop in the rest area off the turnpike, and the other truck was there to receive merchandise in the same manner as last time.

Corey called the DEA agent and alerted him that the operation was a go, then sat back and waited. Last time it took forty-five minutes to make the transfer, and Corey hoped the federal agents would get there a lot sooner than that.

They did.

Eighteen minutes after Corey's call, the place lit up. Corey counted at least eight cars and three larger vehicles. It was hard to see from where he was, but he had no doubt that at least one SWAT team was involved.

Even at that distance, the shouting of the agents could be

heard. One thing that was not heard was any gunfire; there was apparently no resistance.

Corey and his team waited a while to see if anyone escaped the invasion, so that they could go after them. When it became obvious that wasn't to be the case, they moved toward the scene, to learn exactly what was going on. It would be embarrassing if the truck had loaded up with aspirin and deodorant at Winston Pharmaceutical.

Gary Kimbrell, the agent Corey knew within the DEA, saw them arrive and came over to them. Behind him, Corey could see that this had effectively become a mopping-up operation; the passengers of the two trucks were being taken into custody, and the merchandise confiscated.

"You do nice work," Kimbrell said, obviously pleased with the results of the raid. "I assume you don't mind if I take all of the credit for this?"

Corey smiled. "Do I have a choice?"

"Afraid not."

"What did you find?"

"Opioids . . . all kinds. Enough to light up half the western hemisphere. Biggest bust I have ever been involved in."

"Good. Don't forget our deal; we might call on you to testify at our trial."

Kimbrell smiled. "I'll wear my best suit."

Corey called Andy and gave him the good news. Corey had kept him updated periodically on what was going on, but not since the raid began.

Andy put it on the speakerphone so Laurie could hear as well. Corey's recitation of the events was typically detailed and complete.

"Congratulations," Andy said when Corey had finished. "We're going to sleep."

'm going to go against my normal instincts in presenting our case.

I usually like to begin with guns blazing, surprising the jury and using our big guns right from the beginning.

But this time is different. Too many developments are happening outside the courtroom. The key to the case will be in getting Judge Lofton to admit evidence of the criminal conspiracies within Wasserman Equities, and by waiting for things to unfold, I'm hoping to have more ammunition to use.

The news this morning was filled with news of the drug raid last night; the street value of the drugs is estimated at $31 million, an eye-opening number. Neither the media nor the court has any reason to connect the events to our case, but they will soon enough.

All in good time.

It's common knowledge, in my profession and in the real world, that you cannot prove a negative. That is especially true here; there is no way we can ever prove that Tony didn't prepare that chemical and inject Rachel with it.

I wasn't there, the jury wasn't there . . . no one was there except Rachel and her killer.

So we have two approaches. One is to show Tony in the best possible light, to make it seem unlikely that he is a person who would have done something like this. The second, and that will come later, is to present an alternative theory, and an alternative killer.

My first witness is Ray Vaccaro, a close friend of Tony's from Evansville. We've flown him in for this occasion, and he jumped at the opportunity to help.

"How long have you known Mr. Wasserman?" I ask.

"Close to eleven years."

"How did you come to meet?"

"I run a shelter in downtown Evansville. Tony arrived one day and said he wanted to volunteer. At the time we needed all the help we could get, we still do, and we put him right to work."

"So he remained there?"

Vaccaro nods. "Right until the time he came here. Twenty hours a week, at least, and longer in the summer when school was closed."

"Did you ever know him to be violent?"

"Not at all; he's the gentlest person I know."

"A temper?"

"Not that I ever saw."

"What about money? If you know, did that seem important to him?"

"One time Tony came to talk to me, looking for advice. He had been approached to work in private industry, as a research chemist. He asked me what I thought; he said the money was triple what he was working for at the school."

"What did you say?"

"That he should take it. I mean, triple the salary, you know?"

"And what did he decide?"

"That he couldn't do it. That the money wasn't worth leaving his kids."

I keep Vaccaro on the stand a while longer, letting him shower

Tony with more praise, then I turn him over to Strickland. Her treatment of him is designed to show the jury that this testimony is irrelevant, which it mostly is.

"Mr. Vaccaro, do you have any idea who killed Rachel Morehouse?"

"No."

"Do you have any evidence to present to prove it wasn't Anthony Wasserman?"

"Not evidence, but I—"

"Thank you. No further questions," she says, effectively dismissing him.

My next witness is Lorraine Baumann, Rachel's housekeeper. Unless she has a particular fondness for housekeeping, she can stop doing so effective immediately, because Rachel left her $5 million.

After I get her to say that she worked for Stanley well before Rachel came along, then continued on afterward, I ask if she considered Rachel a friend.

"Oh, yes, definitely. I mean, she was my employer, so I respected her in that role, but we were also friends. I liked her very much, and I hope she liked me as well."

"Did she leave you an inheritance in her will?"

"Yes. Five million dollars."

"Did that come as a surprise to you?"

"Oh, yes. I was and am very grateful. I only wish she was here for me to thank her."

"Did you meet Anthony Wasserman?"

"Certainly. He lived in Rachel's house for almost five weeks. I saw a great deal of him."

"Did you see them together?"

"Many times. They ate breakfast and dinner together almost every day, and sometimes lunch as well."

"Did they seem to get along?"

"Yes, definitely. Rachel was very happy that things were going so well between them."

This flies directly in the face of what Susan Wolford had said, so I let this sink in for a while before continuing.

"Did you clean Mr. Wasserman's room?"

She smiles. "A few times, at first. But he asked me not to. He said he's been cleaning his own house his whole life, and it made him uncomfortable for someone else to do it. He didn't think I needed to bother for him."

"Did he do a good job cleaning?"

Another smile. "Not very, no."

"Did you ever see him with any chemicals in the house?"

"No."

"Never saw him mixing chemicals at all?"

"No."

I left her at the stand, and Strickland again asks a few perfunctory questions and dismisses her. The implication is that this testimony is not even worth challenging. It's the proper strategy.

So far I've shown that two people consider Tony a good guy.

I have not shown that he's not a murderer.

James Wolford came home from the office at two o'clock in the afternoon, something he almost never did.

He had told his wife, Susan, that he was on the way home to talk to her, so she was waiting for him.

The day to that point had been an unmitigated disaster, all the result of the drug raid the night before. It wasn't exactly difficult for the media to trace it back to Wasserman Equities, since both the trucking company and the pharmaceutical company were owned by Wasserman.

It had become a public relations catastrophe.

He almost never discussed the business with Susan, but this time there was no avoiding it.

"You read about the drug raid last night?"

"I did. It's terrible how they could do that. You need to fire all of them."

"We hired them. The blame lies with us; the pressure on us is enormous, and it's going to get worse."

"You can ride it out."

"No, and there's more you don't know about. It's where Stanley originally got the money from; they're going to investigate and find out."

Her face reflects her concern. "Oh, no. What are you going to do?"

"I'm going to resign and tell what I know. I don't see another way out."

"Jim, give it time. Maybe it's not as bad as you think."

"Believe me, it is. There is no way out of this. I just don't know how I can face this. I'm sorry, Susan."

With that he went upstairs, leaving her alone in the den.

James Wolford put a gun in his mouth and pulled the trigger. His brains are splattered all over his bedroom."

It's Vince Sanders on the phone, telling me about something that he had just heard and assigned a reporter to cover.

"Are you sure?" This is stunning news, and I react by involuntarily putting my head in both hands. Since I no longer have any hands to hold the phone, it drops to the floor, and I pick it up.

I miss the beginning of Vince's response, but what I hear tells me enough: ". . . thought this might impact your case. You owe me one."

I don't bother telling Vince how much he owes me; instead I get off the phone, call Laurie in to tell her the news, and turn on the television. The story takes about five minutes to hit CNN, and they immediately connect the story to the drug bust.

The question, as they see it, is, How is the parent company connected to these events? In other words, what did Wolford know, and when did he know it?

One pundit also brings up the trial, but he does so in the context of what a rough period Wasserman Equities is going through. "If it was a publicly traded stock," he says, "it would be in free fall right now."

"So what does this mean?" Laurie asks.

"Well, it means that Wolford knew the world was closing in on him. And it means that jail did not have any appeal for him at all."

"I meant for you."

"I've got to admit that my reaction isn't what a horrible trag- edy it is that a life was lost. A lot of lives would have been taken by those opioids. For the case, it's a net plus. When I start to introduce evidence about Wasserman Equities, and Strickland objects, this will bolster my position."

By the time I'm walking the dogs later, I'm somewhat less confident. That bad things were going on at Wasserman Eq- uities does not mean that Tony Wasserman did not kill Rachel Morehouse.

I am going to have to connect the two, or Judge Lofton won't let any of it in. It's that simple.

Court is going to be abbreviated today, concluding with the lunch break. Judge Lofton has some things on his docket that he must deal with. I'm fine with that; I will need to get ready for my trip to the airport with Marcus.

When I arrive in court, Tony asks me about Wolford's suicide and the drug bust. "Does it mean anything for our case?"

"Very possibly; we'll know in the next day or so."

"He must have been involved with the drug dealing?"

"I'm sure he was. Did you ever meet him?"

"No. I met the other guy, Carl Simmons, a couple of times. He came over to talk to Rachel; she didn't like him."

"How do you know that?"

Tony grins. "After he left, she said, 'I can't stand that son of a bitch. I don't trust him, and he likes married women too much.' That tipped me off. Rachel could be direct."

Judge Lofton comes in, and I call Roger Castner to the stand. After I get him to state his name, age, and where he lives, I ask, "Did I ask you to bring something with you to court today?"

"Yes. I have it in my pocket."

"Please take it out."

He reaches into his jacket pocket and takes out a test tube. There is liquid in it, with a stopper so that the liquid cannot leak out.

"What is that?"

"It's potassium chloride."

"Where did you get it?"

"I made it," Castner says with apparent pride. "From scratch."

I introduce as evidence a signed and notarized affidavit from Loretta Naylor, professor of chemistry at Rutgers University. "As you can see, Professor Naylor swears under oath that this is, in fact, potassium chloride, and that she was present while Mr. Castner made it."

Once the document is submitted, I turn back to Castner. "From what university did you earn your degree in chemistry?"

"I don't have one."

"You minored in it?"

"No. I took high school chemistry, but I got a C."

"Are you a self-taught chemist?"

"No."

"What is your occupation, Mr. Castner?"

"I'm the baseball coach at Fairleigh Dickinson University. So the only chemistry I've ever worried about is team chemistry."

I feign bewilderment. "So did Professor Naylor teach you how to make the potassium chloride?"

"No, she just watched me."

"How did you learn how to do it?"

"I googled it. There are a bunch of videos that explain it really clearly."

"How long did it take you?"

He thinks for a few moments, trying to remember. "Well, I

watched the video twice to make sure I remembered it all. And then, the process itself . . . I guess the whole thing took about fifteen or twenty minutes. I could have done it faster, but I was being really careful."

Strickland's questioning is once again brief. "Mr. Castner, did you leave any of the chemical you made in Anthony Wasserman's bedroom?"

"No."

"In his car?"

"No."

"Were you upset when Rachel Morehouse did not leave you her fortune in her will?"

"No. I didn't think she even considered me."

The jury and gallery laugh at the response, not the reaction Strickland was looking for. She lets him off the stand, and Judge Lofton determines that not enough time is left for another witness before lunch, so we're out of here.

I head home to watch coverage of the Wolford suicide, work on strategy for the rest of the defense case, and look over the list that Sam gave me of people that the Wasserman Equities–owned headhunting firm has placed in jobs in the last three years.

Then I have to prepare for my airport date with Marcus tonight.

I already know what Masterson Aviation Airport looks like. Sam took detailed photos and sent them to me, and I shared them with Marcus.

But even if Sam hadn't, we could have gotten the lay of the land quickly, even in the night darkness.

It's basically one building and one runway. I don't see an air traffic control tower anywhere; they must use the services of Newark Airport. We don't go into the building, but Sam's photos had told us that it's just a waiting area that could accommodate maybe fifteen people, some vending machines, and a desk where people check in and out.

Passengers use a door to the left of the desk to get out to the runway, and currently three cars are in the small parking lot outside the building. No one seems to be around, so maybe those cars are here overnight, or more likely they will used by the people on the arriving plane.

That assumes I'm right and there is an arriving plane. My theory is that the incoming Global Aviation planes don't go direct to Newark, but instead make an unauthorized stop here first.

The entire place seems to be surrounded by a five-foot-high chain-link fence. One area, maybe two hundred feet long, is tree-lined, and that's where we position ourselves. It will give us a pretty good view of a plane once it taxis to the building, and the building itself.

At ten thirteen, we can see and hear a plane in the distance, heading our way. A few minutes later it's on the ground, taxiing toward the building. It comes within about fifty feet, and I can see it looks like it's a jet that could seat about twenty, but I know nothing about planes so I'm just guessing.

The door opens and the stairs roll down automatically. Two people get off the plane; I'm not sure if one is the pilot. A third person, who I did not realize was in the building, comes out to greet them. They talk briefly, but I can't hear what they are saying.

"Enjoying the view?"

A jolt of fear goes through my body, and Marcus and I turn and see a man standing in the darkness, moonlight reflecting off a gun in his hand. I also think I see that Marcus is holding his own gun, but in a swift motion he puts it in his pocket. I would prefer he'd use it to shoot this guy.

Neither Marcus nor I answer. I don't because I am too scared to speak, and Marcus never even answers me, so he is sure as hell not going to answer this stranger.

"Put your hands on the fence and spread out," he says, and we both do so. I have never known Marcus to be so compliant.

The guy frisks us and finds Marcus's gun, which he puts in his own pocket. "Let's move. We're going for a ride." He's not the most talkative guy in the world, but he's carrying the whole conversation.

He marches us to the building and then inside. Then we go out the door to the plane and walk to it. "Up the stairs."

Once we get inside, I see that there are only ten seats. They're plush and comfortable looking, but I'm not anxious to get in one. What I'd really like to happen is what always seems to happen when I travel: my flight gets canceled.

A man I assume to be the pilot is still on the plane, waiting for us to board, and holding a handgun. The original guy comes up the stairs behind us, so now two guns are trained on us. Once we're all in, the original guy says, "Take a seat . . . there and there."

I sit on the left and Marcus on the right. While the pilot holds the gun on us, the original guy handcuffs Marcus to the right armrest, and me to the armrest to my left.

"Comfortable?" the original guy asks, though I don't think he actually cares about our comfort.

My concern is Marcus, who has been unusually docile this whole time. I have never seen him allow himself to be put into this situation; and the obvious problem is that I am counting on him to save us.

The original guy goes up into the cockpit, where the pilot has just started the engines. My fear, and it's making me literally ache, is that the plan is for this to be a one-way trip for us.

I see Marcus looking at the armrest and handcuffs, almost like he's testing them out. I do the same, but I have no idea why I'm doing it, and I'm not encouraged by the results.

Suddenly we speed down the runway and are in the air. I look out the window, and it is only a few minutes before I stop seeing lights below; there is only blackness. I have no doubt we are over the ocean, which elevates my fear level to DEFCON 1.

The cockpit door opens and the original guy and pilot both come out. This time the pilot is the only one carrying a gun. "Time to go for a little swim," the original guy says.

They walk toward us, the pilot staying three or four feet behind him, so the other seats won't get in the way if he has to shoot us.

The original guy takes what looks like a key out of his pocket. "You first," he says to me, and walks toward me. I have not said one word since we were snuck up on outside, and I'm unable to form one now.

As he leans over to undo the handcuff, his face seems to explode in red as it is smashed into by something. I recoil from it before I realize that it is an armrest that has turned his face to mush. It sure as hell isn't my armrest, so it must be Marcus's.

Everyone . . . the pilot, me, and the guy with the crushed face, is shocked and slow to react. Everyone except for Marcus. He is already out of his seat and throws the original guy, who must weigh 230 pounds, back at the pilot, like he was tossing a beanbag.

The pilot backs off and his gun fires, but the bullet goes wildly off to the left, into one of the seats. Marcus is on him in a split second. I realize that he is still handcuffed to the armrest; I guess it proved weaker than the handcuffs.

But it doesn't matter either way. Marcus takes the armrest and hits the pilot over the head with it. Then again. And again. Apparently, the fact that these people were planning to dump Marcus into the ocean annoyed him.

The pilot goes to the floor. If he is alive, his skull must be made of titanium. I look at the mass of blood and gore that used to be his head. I can't tell if he's still breathing, but I have no tremendous interest in finding out. And there is no way I am giving him mouth to mouth.

While I am relieved that I'm not falling headfirst into the ocean, we have one little problem we haven't accounted for.

The guy with the crushed head is the pilot.

Marcus, that's the pilot!" are the first, unnecessary words that come out of my mouth, followed by "Who the hell is going to land this plane?"

If Marcus is concerned, or if he even heard me, I would never know it by his actions. He goes to the original guy, lying there with the smashed-in face. Marcus rolls him over so that he's facedown, which is fine with me.

But Marcus wasn't doing it because he was squeamish; he rolled him over because the handcuff key was on the floor under him. Marcus takes the key and frees himself from the detached armrest. Then he leans over and uncuffs me as well.

"Marcus, who is going to land this plane?"

I know I'm talking; I can hear myself. But Marcus isn't responding. All he's doing is heading toward the cockpit. I take one last cringing look at the two guys lying on the floor; if we're counting on one of them to get up and literally bail us out, we're in deep shit.

The idea of bailing out has some merit, though I would be way too scared to try it unless faced with death. On the other hand, since death is what we are literally faced with, I decide to look for parachutes. I run around the plane accomplishing nothing, then head for the cockpit to see if any are in there. I would also like to find out what the hell Marcus is doing.

As I reach the cockpit, I hear someone say something about a throttle, and I realize it is coming through a radio. Then I hear another voice say, "We're going to need authorization to land, and a clear runway. Wouldn't hurt to have emergency crews standing by."

It's Marcus.

Marcus is talking normally, saying complete, comprehensible words in complete, comprehensible sentences.

We must have flown into another dimension.

"We'll need ambulances on-site," Marcus continues. "There are two assailants, possibly deceased, I haven't had time to confirm."

The earlier sentences were obviously not a fluke; Marcus is still talking. All I can do is watch as Marcus manages the controls, acting as if he knows what he is doing. I hope he's not acting.

"Go sit down and put your seat belt on," he says to me. "Brace yourself; I haven't done this in a while."

I am too stunned to do anything but go in the back and do as he says. I want to sit in the seat farthest in the back, under the theory that planes don't back into mountains. But that would mean climbing over the two bloody bodies, and possibly looking at them. So instead I take the seat in the front. I put my seat belt on and wait.

I can feel the plane turning gradually, nothing jarring, and soon I see the lights of civilization down below. My ears start to clog slightly, indicating a descent, and then I hear the landing gear start to lower. It all feels so normal I almost expect an announcement over the speaker telling me to put my seat back and tray tables up.

I grab the armrests as tightly as I can, though it's hard to imagine that would do the trick to save me if we crash. As we approach the ground, my anxiety increases so much that I might be yelling, or maybe not . . . I can't tell.

Suddenly, the wheels hit the ground, and now I know for sure that I am screaming. I look out the window and see trucks and lights and equipment and people everywhere, but we are gliding right past them. And we're slowing down! And now we're stopped!

Marcus comes out of the cockpit, presses a button, the door opens, and the stairs come down. He motions for me to stay where I am, which is a smart move, because police come running up the steps, guns drawn. One of them looks at the two guys on the floor and says, "Holy shit."

They take us into custody, and we are brought into one of the buildings on the airport grounds. Only then do I realize we're at Teterboro Airport, which is in Bergen County and only about a dozen miles from Manhattan. I guess that's where the authorities thought they could most easily deal with whatever is going on.

I see that Corey Douglas is here, along with a few state cops that I recognize and Corey knows well. I think every conceivable government agency is represented, from the FBI to the ATF to the FAA. I wouldn't be surprised if the Farm Bureau is here as well; the government is taking this very seriously.

Laurie shows up about a half hour later; I assume she dropped Ricky off at Will Rubenstein's house. But neither she nor Corey can talk to us for a long while; we are questioned endlessly by various guys in suits.

For a while I am afraid we are going to be taken into custody, but we're not. At 2:15 A.M. we're told that we're free to go; I don't know if it's Corey's connections or something else they've learned that makes them realize we are okay, and that we're the victims, not the perpetrators.

Finally I'm on the way home with Laurie, and I relate to her what happened, in chronological order.

"He talked, Laurie. He talked normally, no grunting, and no needing subtitles to understand what he was saying. Like I'm talking to you, that's how he was talking on the plane."

She nods knowingly.

"Did you know he could do that?"

"Yes. He only shows that side to certain people; he thinks he gets more out of people thinking he can't communicate effectively. I'm not sure why, but I've never questioned it. You're now in the club."

"Why didn't you tell me?"

"He didn't want me to."

"And did you know he could fly a plane?"

"Not for sure, but I do know he was once in the air force. I suspect there's a lot about Marcus that we don't know."

"He pulled an armrest right out of the seat. It was unbelievable."

"That doesn't surprise me at all."

"I think he wanted us to be discovered. He wasn't happy with my plan to just watch and see what happened. He just thinks he can handle any situation that arises."

Another nod from Laurie. "The good news is that he can."

The news of the night's events has exploded in the media, but I don't have time to watch much of it. I need to get to court.

I'm certain that based on what Judge Lofton must already know about what happened, I could get a continuance if I asked for it. Certainly he would call off the morning session, and most likely the whole day, if I made the request.

But I don't want to. I want to strike while the news is fresh, and I also want to get a foundational witness in before I do so.

When I arrive at court, Eddie Dowd and Tony ask me questions about what happened, but the session is about to start, so I don't have time to say much. Strickland comes over, smiles, and says, "You have an interesting life."

My opening witness today is Ronald Rugoff, the former CFO of Wasserman Equities. Laurie had interviewed him and thought he would be helpful for what we are trying to accomplish.

Rugoff had been the CFO at Wasserman Equities for three years; Stanley Wasserman hired him, and he was let go soon after Stanley's death. I'm not sure if Rugoff knows where the original money backing Wasserman came from, but either way he would not be about to admit it. He doesn't have to; it's hidden behind enough shell companies that no one could prove anything.

Once I establish who he is and what his job had been, I say, "I'd like to talk to you today about Rachel Morehouse. You knew her?"

"Certainly."

"Were you personal friends?"

"No, I strictly knew her through the business, though we attended some of the same industry events and charity functions when her husband was alive."

"Did she take much of an interest in the business when Stanley Wasserman was alive?"

"I honestly can't say, but if she did, I didn't know about it."

"And after he died?"

"I would describe her interest as intense."

"Why do you say that?"

"She kept calling me and asking me questions about the business and about things that had happened while I was there."

"Only about the parent company?"

"No, about the acquired businesses as well. It was as if she was trying to understand something specific or prove some kind of point."

"But you don't know what that was?"

"No, she never shared that with me."

"Why didn't she go through the co-CEOs, James Wolford or Carl Simmons, or the current CFO?"

"I don't know that either, but she made me promise that I would not tell any of them what she was doing."

"And did you comply with her request?"

He nods. "I did. I no longer have any connection with those people anyway. And I don't exactly consider them close friends; they let me go for no good reason. I was doing my job effectively."

I take a shot here on a hunch and ask a question I don't know how he will answer. It's a cardinal sin for an attorney, but there's no answer that can badly hurt us, and I'd like to hear how he answers it under oath.

"Did she indicate which of the two co-CEOs she was more interested in, in terms of their actions and job performance?"

"She didn't say so directly, but my sense based on her questions was that she was more focused on Mr. Simmons."

"Thank you. No further questions."

I've made my point effectively, even if the jury doesn't quite understand it yet. Strickland understands it quite well and attempts to undermine it.

"Mr. Rugoff, you testified that, to your knowledge, Rachel Morehouse had little involvement with the business prior to her husband's death?"

"To my knowledge, that's true."

"When he passed away, she effectively became the owner?"

"Yes."

"Would you find it unusual that the owner of a business would want to understand it?"

"Certainly not."

"Was Rachel Morehouse the person that installed Mr. Wolford and Mr. Simmons in their jobs?"

"No, Stanley. . . . Mr. Wasserman . . . did that."

"Would you describe it as unusual that a new owner would want to make an independent judgment about the people running her company?"

"No, I wouldn't."

"Did she ever allege any criminality?"

"Not to me."

"Did she imply anything nefarious was happening?"

"I can't say that one way or the other. She wasn't confiding in me; she was using me as a source of information."

"So let me recap, and please tell me if I am stating this correctly. A woman inherited a large company that to your knowledge she previously had limited or no involvement in. She then set out to learn about the company and the people that were running it. Is that accurate?"

"Seems to be."

"Thank you."

Next I call Gerald Bridges, the reporter who works for Vince. He testifies that Rachel kept promising a big story, and that he is sure it was about the business. He thought that it involved dirty money.

"So she was intensely trying to find wrongdoing that she felt was rampant in the company?"

Bridges nods. "That's certainly what it seemed like to me."

"Thank you."

Corey and Laurie are both at the courthouse during lunch to brief me on what they've learned in the last few hours about what happened last night.

There isn't that much, and what they have found out is so far unofficial.

"The guy who came up behind you at the airport, Roy Callison, is pretty much a duplicate of the drive-by shooter, Marrero," says Corey.

"What do you mean by *duplicate?*"

"Just like Marrero, he lived in two cities, in this case Atlanta and Chicago. He claimed to be a truck driver, but wasn't. He had no job and no obvious source of income, but had all the money he needed. By the way, he's alive."

"Really?"

Laurie nods. "His modeling career is probably over, unless the smashed-in-face look becomes a thing. But it looks like he will make it. They haven't been able to question him yet."

"Don't tell me the pilot is alive also?"

"No," says Corey. "It turns out that Marcus swings a mean armrest. Go figure."

"They were going to drop us out of that plane, so I'm having trouble feeling sorry for either of them. Who was the pilot?"

"He was from Croatia and served in their air force. He was

arrested for smuggling four years ago and put in prison, but he escaped, apparently with help. He hadn't been seen since."

"And Callison?"

"He has a full history, but so far it seems fake. Obviously the investigation has a long way to go."

"There's something you need to try and find out," I say. "Last night, when the plane landed, two guys got off. They were met by a third guy. I want to know if there is any trace of them, and whether they were listed on the flight manifest. The plane was supposed to go to Newark. I doubt you'll find their names any-where, but that would be significant in itself."

I learned much of what I needed to know last night. I knew that the Global Aviation planes coming in from Portugal could not have been empty, which is how Sam said they were always listed. But I couldn't be positive whether they were carrying some kind of contraband or people.

The answer, quite obviously, was people.

"Laurie, we're going to need to meet with people from Home-land Security. Call Agent Bracey in the Newark office of the FBI; I met with her earlier about trying to find the source of Wasserman's dirty money. Tell her it's an urgent matter of na-tional security; if she resists at all, call Cindy Spodek and ask her to set it up. I want them here at the end of the court day; if you have to, threaten them that this is their only chance to hear what's going on."

"You want to tell us what is actually going on?"

"I can't now; I'm late to get back to court. But I will later."

The afternoon court session will be by far the most crucial so far because it will determine whether Judge Lofton will give me the freedom to present our case the way I want to present it.

I have two ways I can handle it: I can anticipate that our

approach will be hotly contested, and I can call for a hearing outside the presence of the jury to fight it out.

Or I can just go ahead and start, at which point Strickland will object and we'll still fight it out.

Option one looks like I'm concerned and feel the keep-it-out argument might have some merit. Option two looks like I have no concern and can't imagine how anyone can object.

I'm going with option two.

Full speed ahead.

We call Gary Kimbrell."

Gary Kimbrell, the DEA agent that Corey hand delivered the huge drug bust, is here to fulfill his promise to testify. I have one eye on him and one on Strickland; the over/under on how long it is going to take her to object is about four minutes.

"Mr. Kimbrell, what is your occupation?" I ask innocently enough.

"I am an agent in the Drug Enforcement Administration."

"You try and stop people from trafficking in illegal drugs?"

He nods. "That's an important part of my job, yes."

"Did a member of my investigative team, Corey Douglas, contact you recently?"

"He did."

"What did he tell you?"

"That there was an illegal drug operation going on, one that was on a very large scale."

"Objection," says Strickland, beating the over/under number by forty-five seconds. "May we approach?"

"You may."

Strickland and I head for the bench, speaking out of the earshot of the jury. "Your Honor, as I feared and predicted, Mr. Carpenter is attempting to take us all on a fantasy fishing trip."

I start to answer, but Judge Lofton cuts me off. "I'll hear both sides, but let's get the jury out of here first."

I'm already pleased with how this is going. Our arguments will take place in front of the gallery and assembled media; I want this reported widely tomorrow.

The judge sends us back to our respective tables as the jury files out. Once they're gone, he asks Strickland to state her objection. She stands to do so.

"Your Honor, Mr. Carpenter is about to introduce evidence of crimes that have absolutely nothing to do with the case we are trying. His apparent belief is that if he throws enough against the wall, the jury might not understand that all that he is saying is irrelevant.

"He has made no offer of proof that these outside incidents bear in any way on the murder of Rachel Morehouse. The reason he has not is that he cannot, because it doesn't."

"Mr. Carpenter?"

"Your Honor, our intention is to present facts. Witnesses like Agent Kimbrell and others will do just that. Those facts, when taken together, will prove beyond any reasonable doubt that there was . . . there is . . . a criminal conspiracy directed by Wasserman Equities.

"A number of people, not just Rachel Morehouse, have died in service of this conspiracy. Most of them were murdered. One of them, co-CEO James Wolford, took his own life when the incident that Agent Kimbrell is about to testify to took place.

"It is absurd that in this environment the jury should be encased in so airtight a bubble that the information we have is not presented. They need to hear it and judge it. Ms. Strickland can offer them her countertheories, and they can decide who is right."

We fight some more, basically rehashing the same points. I

don't think there is a serious possibility we are going to lose this debate. First of all, most rational people would see at least the possibility of a connection between these criminal and violent events and the case we are trying.

Second, the gathered media are mostly composed of rational people, and most important, so are the judges who sit on the court of appeals. Judge Lofton has to know that there is at least a significant chance he could be overturned on appeal if he rules against us and the jury convicts. Judges quite naturally hate outcomes like that.

But Judge Lofton can throw Strickland one bone, and he throws it. "You can proceed, Mr. Carpenter . . . the prosecution objection is overruled. But I will be monitoring it carefully, and if I find that you are going too far afield and raising matters not related to the case we are trying, I will put a stop to it immediately."

The jury comes back in and Agent Kimbrell retakes the stand. I take him through the mechanics of what took place the other night, and how they conducted the raid.

Then, "If you know, who owns Winston Pharmaceutical, where the opioids originated?"

"Wasserman Equities."

"And whose truck made the pickup?"

"National Trucking."

"If you know, who owns National Trucking?"

"Wasserman Equities."

"Thank you."

Strickland gets up, a fake look of anger on her face. I have no idea if the jurors recognize it as fake; they probably don't.

"Agent Kimbrell, who killed Rachel Morehouse?"

"I have no idea; I haven't followed the case or this trial."

"Do you have any evidence at all that the incident you are

describing the other night—and by the way we thank you for all you do to protect us—do you have any evidence that the incident has anything to do with this trial?"

"I do not."

"Not a shred?"

"I have no such evidence, but—"

Strickland cuts him off. "Thank you."

"The witness should be allowed to finish this answer," I say.

Judge Lofton nods and turns to Kimbrell. "You may finish your answer."

"I was just going to say that while I don't have such evidence, I also haven't looked for any."

My next witness is Samantha Reisinger, the widow of Matt Reisinger, who we firmly believe was pushed over a cliff in North Carolina three years ago.

Reisinger was the CEO of Global Aviation, the company whose plane I had the misfortune of flying in last night. I don't care how many frequent-flier miles I earned, I am never getting back on one of their planes again.

We flew Samantha in from Cincinnati last night. If I've ever been around a witness more eager to testify, I can't remember when. Of course, that doesn't mean she was willing to fly coach; she has her standards.

She wears black to court, not because I told her to, but I think she consulted the grieving widow's fashion handbook. I had to caution her not to overplay it, to just answer my questions straightforwardly. She is just a setup witness for us; the main event is to follow.

Once I've established her name and that she lives in Cincinnati, I ask, "Your husband was Matthew Reisinger?"

"Yes. He passed away three years ago."

"He ran Global Aviation?"

"Yes. He was the president and CEO. He started the company from scratch and then eventually sold it to Wasserman Equities."

"And made a lot of money in the sale?"

"Yes, but it was still the worst mistake he ever made. There were problems there after they took over, and he was upset about them. He was going to deal with them."

"Did he tell you what the problems were?"

"No, I wish he had. He always tried to protect me. And then he died before he could do what he planned to do."

"What was the cause of death?"

"He was thrown off a cliff while on a hiking trip in the North Carolina mountains."

"You say he was thrown off a cliff? Did the police rule it a murder?"

"Not back then; they called it an accidental death."

"Why did you disagree?"

"Matt was an incredibly experienced outdoorsman. He taught courses in outdoor safety. I've been hiking with him; there is no way he would put himself in any kind of dangerous position."

"And you told that to the police?"

"Yes. They wouldn't listen. It was horrible, to know that your husband was murdered and to have no one in authority believe you."

"Do you know the name Stephen Gilley?"

She nods. "Yes. I knew Stephen."

"What can you tell us about him?"

"Stephen worked for Matt; he was vice president in charge of public relations. They were very close."

"Was he there when your husband died?"

"He left after it happened. He didn't give notice or anything; he just left town and disappeared. No one knew where he went . . . except me."

"You were in contact with him?"

"He called me. He told me that he could never come back,

that he knew too much. He said he was sorry, but Matt was gone and nothing would bring him back."

"You knew how to reach him?"

"Yes, but he asked me never to call unless I needed him. He was scared to death."

"Did I come to see you weeks ago?"

"Yes. You told me you believed Matt was murdered, and that it tied into the business. You were the first person to believe me."

"What did you do?"

"I called Stephen and told him about you. I said that this was the answer; he could tell you everything and you would take it from there. He wouldn't have to expose himself to danger."

"Where is Stephen Gilley today?"

Samantha starts to cry, and Judge Lofton offers to take a break if she needs it. "No, thank you, I want to get through this." Then, "Stephen is dead. They killed him."

"And did the police tell you this?"

"Yes. And they told me my phone was tapped. That's how the killers found him." She starts to cry again. "I caused Stephen's death. We both did."

Strickland's cross-examination of Samantha is gentle; you don't push grieving widows around, even if they've been grieving for three years and their testimony is hurting your case.

All she does is what she has been doing; she gets Samantha to say that not only did she know nothing about who murdered Rachel Morehouse, but she had never heard of Rachel until recently.

Judge Lofton gavels the court day to a close, and I see in the rear of the courtroom that Laurie is here with Agent Bracey of the FBI. I don't see anyone else with them, which is a major disappointment.

Apparently, the US government is not intimidated by the threats of Andy Carpenter, attorney at law.

Only Agent Bracey has shown up, and she seems pissed to be here.

Laurie, Bracey, and I go into an anteroom to talk in private. "You're the only one coming?"

"You're lucky I'm here. I wouldn't be if Agent Spodek hadn't said you're to be taken seriously."

"I said this was an urgent matter of national security."

"So tell me, and I'll tell the president."

I'm officially annoyed at her attitude, and the attitude of the people at Homeland Security who didn't consider this important enough to be here.

"Okay, then we'll make this brief. I am aware of a conspiracy which represents a major threat to this country. It is like a national time bomb that could go off at any time."

"You want to be more specific?" Bracey asks.

"Actually, I don't. Instead I want to dictate the terms of our agreement."

"You're dictating terms?" Her tone is bemused, further annoying me. I'm getting cranky in my old age.

"Right. I'll tell you what is going on in return for a promise that someone in Homeland Security will testify to it at this trial."

"There is no way anyone will agree to that without having some idea what the hell you are talking about."

"The lack of trust hurts me very deeply."

"So let's hear it."

"No. We'll do it another way. You know who Chris Marrero and Roy Callison are?" I hope she's been following this case and the news enough to know that they are the two people who tried to kill me. Callison's name was all over the media this morning because he was one of the people on the plane last night.

She nods. "I know who they are."

I take a piece of paper out of my pocket and hand it to her. "Here are the names of five people. I've included where they live and where they work."

She looks at the paper and then back at me. "So?"

"So check out their backgrounds. And I don't mean a cursory check; I mean do a deep dive like was done with Marrero and Callison."

"And then what?"

"And then agree to my deal. You have two days."

"That's all you want me to tell my people?"

"No, tell your people that this country is being invaded, and they better get their heads out of their asses before it's too late."

Bracey turns to Laurie. "Is he always this obnoxious?"

Laurie shrugs. "He's usually quite charming."

My threat may or may not succeed. If I had to bet, I'd say it will, and that the government will give in to my demand. But at its core, the threat is empty.

That's because at the end of the day I will tell what I know, or at least what I strongly suspect. I'll have to; I couldn't live with the potential consequences if I didn't.

But either way, I'm not counting on the government to ride into the courtroom on a white horse, testify, and save the day. Our case will have to stand or fall on its own.

Laurie and I head home. We have dinner, then walk the dogs together, and have a glass of wine in the den when we get back. I'm exhausted, crashing; the events of last night on the plane have affected me more than I realized. I've been in dangerous situations before, and I've hated every one of them, but last night was different. It was by far the most frightening thing I have ever experienced.

"I thought I was going to die in the ocean," I say. "I found myself wondering if I would die from the impact on hitting the water, or drown."

"Andy . . ."

"I was so scared I was even doubting Marcus."

"You think of yourself as a coward. But anyone in that situation would react that way."

"Except Marcus."

She nods, smiling. "Except Marcus."

"I thought he was turning into Clark Kent in front of my eyes."

"You going to stay up and prepare for court tomorrow?"

"No, I'm ready."

"Then let's go to bed."

I nod. "That works."

Captain John Everton of the New York State Police is probably not thrilled to be here.

Police officers are just not used to testifying for the defense in a trial; it instinctively goes against their grain. Even though he had nothing to do with arresting Tony, or with this case at all, he would naturally feel that if Tony was arrested, he's almost definitely guilty.

But I've called him because he is the person who can most credibly testify to the incident at the Red Apple Rest Stop, and that testimony is crucial to our case.

But as important as Everton is, our star witness comes next. We're going to call Carl Simmons, the only remaining CEO now that James Wolford is dead.

I'm going to prepare like hell for that tonight, and then tomorrow I am going to attack Simmons and blame him for everything but the Kennedy assassination. And if I can find any evidence that he's been to Dallas, I may nail him for that as well.

But for now I have to focus on Everton, and I bring him back to that night at the Red Apple.

"Captain, did you get a call from my investigator Corey Douglas that night?"

"Yes."

"Had you known Corey from his time as a cop in Paterson?"

"Yes, we had occasion to work on a case together a number of years ago."

"So you trust him?"

"Completely."

"What did he tell you when he called?"

"That he was at the Red Apple Rest Stop, in Tuxedo, off Route Seventeen. It's now an abandoned building, but used to be a popular restaurant for travelers along that road. He said a murder had been committed there."

"So what did you do?"

"I called in backup and went there immediately."

"What did you find when you arrived?"

"Corey was there, as were you and another investigator named Marcus Clark. Corey's police dog was there as well. You were inside the building, and there was a body there as well. He was deceased."

"How did that person die?"

"Multiple stab wounds. Well more than would have been necessary to cause his death."

"Was the deceased killed in the building, if you know?"

"No, the investigation showed that he was killed in the nearby woods and dragged into the building."

"Please tell us the name of the victim."

"Stephen Gilley."

Just to make sure that the jurors don't have their heads up their asses, I ask Everton if he is aware of Samantha Reisinger's testimony that Gilley had been afraid for his life and had fled after Matt Reisinger was killed.

Everton confirms all that and talks about the contact he'd had with the Cincinnati police.

"So Mr. Gilley had worked for Global Aviation? Owned by Wasserman Equities?"

"Yes."

"Do you have an opinion as to why Mr. Gilley's body was dragged into the building and not just left in the forest?"

"I believe it was to send you a message to see when you arrived to meet him."

"What kind of message?"

"That you should stop investigating, or it could happen to you."

"Stop investigating this case?"

Strickland objects that Everton could not know what was in the killer's mind, and that he shouldn't be speculating about it. She should have objected three questions ago; she was too slow on the trigger.

Judge Lofton sustains the objection, and I have no more questions for Everton.

I only half listen to Strickland's cross, during which she again points to the lack of direct connection to the murder of Rachel Morehouse.

My mind is already on tomorrow, and how I am going to attack Carl Simmons.

'm in the den preparing for my direct examination of Carl Simmons when Laurie comes into the room.

"Turn on CNN." Her tone tells me there is something on there that I'm not going to like.

I reach for the remote. "What's going on?"

"Carl Simmons has been arrested."

The story is on as "breaking news," and it's not exactly filled with details. The gist of it is that Simmons has been arrested on drug-trafficking charges, related to the bust that was made on the Pennsylvania Turnpike the other night.

I can only assume that the authorities have investigated and have firmly tied him to it. I don't know what evidence they've uncovered, or how strong their case is, but there is one thing I know for sure.

This is a disaster for us.

I needed Simmons on the stand to tie everything together. I had an embarrassment of riches to attack him with, and now I can't use any of it. And it's not like he's been arrested for the murder of Rachel Morehouse, or for that matter any other homicides.

He's been arrested for drug trafficking, which will not impress our jury, if they're even allowed to hear it.

I am going to have to ask for a continuance in the morning. I expect that Judge Lofton will grant it. He knows that Simmons was my next witness; I had announced it to the court. He also knows that it's not my fault that Simmons is unavailable; he is currently being held pending an arraignment tomorrow.

Laurie and I call everyone we know to try to get an update on what the hell is going on. I call Pete Stanton, and Vince Sanders, and Corey Douglas and ask if they have any information. They all promise to see what they can find out.

By the end of the night we've learned that the arrest is, in fact, limited to the drug trafficking. Apparently the money from previous drug activity has been traced back to Wasserman Equities and Simmons in particular.

The company will be charged as well, though no other executives are expected to be indicted criminally.

Simmons had surrendered in an arrangement between his attorneys and the DEA; apparently this had been in the works for a few days. There is talk that he might tell what he knows in a plea deal, though that is far from certain.

This is potentially devastating for our case, and extremely depressing. Then, just as Laurie and I are about to go to sleep, the phone rings. It's Agent Bracey of the FBI.

Her message is short, but sweet. "You've got a deal."

The criminal justice god giveth, and he taketh away.

Judge Lofton granted the continuance until tomorrow, which is why I am able to be in Agent Bracey's office for a 10:00 A.M. meeting.

I was going to bring Laurie and Corey to this meeting, but I need them to spend their time learning as much as they can about the Carl Simmons situation. So only Eddie Dowd accompanies me.

This time they are out in some force. We're introduced to an assistant director of Homeland Security and another FBI suit, who I suspect is Bracey's boss. It's the Homeland Security guy, Peter Unser, who does the talking.

Unser comes right to the point. "If your information is what it appears to be, we will so testify in your trial."

I have no choice but to take him at his word, since I am going to tell them what I know anyway.

"Good. Global Aviation flights have been coming in periodically from Portugal," I say. "But I'm confident that Portugal is not where they originated from. My guess is that they come from Russia, but I can't be sure. I have no doubt you can find that out.

"When the plane lands in Portugal, no one disembarks, so there is no need for them to go through customs there. Portugal is used as a departure point strictly to deceive.

"The flights are listed as empty of passengers or cargo; they are allegedly coming in strictly to return the plane to the US, so that they can be put back into passenger service. They are always scheduled to land at Newark Airport, and always at ten fifteen at night.

"But they are not empty, and their first stop is never Newark. They are carrying people, just a few at a time, and they stop first at Masterson Aviation, and then on to Newark. I believe that if you investigate, they must be paying off a specific air traffic controller at Newark, who is always on at that time, and who fixes the records to allow for the diversion and the fifty-five-minute delay in getting to Newark."

"And the passengers get off at Masterson?" Unser asks.

"Yes. I saw that for myself the other night. These are people that are not American, though I don't know their nationality. They have been given American identities, all ingeniously created in cyberspace. Wasserman has a computer company, but I don't know if they are involved. My guess is it is all done overseas.

"Wasserman has a headhunting company that places these people in jobs. The jobs are at various levels, but all in key industries and elements of the country's infrastructure. The names I gave you are in transportation, power, and finance, and there are a lot more besides them. You can start with these.

"There is no need for the adversaries to hack into these systems because they now have people in place. It does not take someone in a key position to leave a computer system open to invasion; it can be done by something as simple as opening a virus-filled email. I don't have to tell you that.

"Basically, there is an invasion force, sitting like Manchurian candidates, waiting to shut down our grids, or stop our financial system from functioning, or conducting the mother of all ransomware attacks. You will find the names and locations of these people in the Wasserman company files."

"Where does the drug trafficking come in?" Bracey's boss asks.

I shrug. "I think it's for financing their operations. They bought companies that they could use for criminal activities. There is probably much more going on that we don't yet know about."

They have more questions, most of which I can't answer. Finally Unser says, "How does this help you with your murder case?"

It's a good question, and one I hope the jury does not focus on. "I have been making the point that Wasserman Equities is one massive criminal conspiracy. The government testifying to that effect will clinch the deal."

Unser nods. "We'll be there."

At 3:00 A.M. I hear the beep of a text message on my phone. The chance of it being good news is pretty slim, so I get up to look, hoping it's some spam message that my car needs servicing or a new warranty.

It's from Unser at Homeland Security, and he didn't look like the type that cares one way or another about my car. His message is short but ominous: *Be at the courthouse a half hour early. We have to talk.*

Thus ends the sleep portion of the night for me. I text him back, asking what is going on, but he doesn't respond. Unlike me, he's probably already sleeping like a baby.

I take the dogs for a 6:00 A.M. walk, which Tara and Hunter are fine with, but which annoys Sebastian to no end. He doesn't even want to be awake, much less on the move. But he takes one for the team and joins us.

I drop them off, shower and dress, and get to the courthouse on time, only to find out that Unser is already waiting for me, which is another bad sign.

We go into the anteroom, and he gets right to it. "I want to update you on some things. First of all, Simmons is cutting a deal."

"Already?"

"Yes. He claims he knows it's over for him, and he wants to

come clean. I think he wants to avoid the death penalty, since he's being tried federally. His crimes go way across state lines.

"Anyway, he's copping to the drug stuff and to the killings, though he says he only knew of them; he didn't authorize or commit them himself. He also admits to bringing people into the country illegally on the Global Aviation planes, although he says he did not know what the purpose was. He says they were just paid a lot of money to do it."

"He's trying to avoid a treason charge."

Unser nods. "That's my view also. He also says he was just taking orders; that he was dealing with someone called Stal."

"Are you familiar with him?"

"Unfortunately, yes. He is not someone you want to run into."

"Where is Simmons now?"

"At home on two million dollar bail, wearing an electronic monitor. When the deal is finalized and murder is added to the charge, bail will be revoked and he'll be taken back into custody."

"Is that it?" I instinctively know that it isn't. Unser has not dropped the bad-news bomb yet; he didn't come here early to update me on Simmons. I ask another question I know the answer to. "Will Simmons testify in our trial?"

"No, and I'm afraid I can't either."

"You gave me your word."

"I know, and I'm sorry . . . truly. But rounding up the people that were brought in and placed in jobs is going to take a while, and it has to be done at once so that it's a surprise. Otherwise they could initiate an action against our country before we can get to them, before they know we're onto them."

"So?"

"So it has to be a secret, which means I can't talk about it."

"But you—"

"Andy, last night the president classified the entire operation. If I were to testify to it, I would be committing treason myself." A pause. "And I'm afraid the same thing is true of you."

"No one can stop me from defending my client."

"Andy, the president . . ." Unser doesn't finish the sentence; he doesn't have to. "And the bottom line is that my testimony couldn't help you anyway. So they brought people into the country and placed them in significant jobs; does that mean your client is innocent?" He doesn't wait for me to answer. "And there's one more thing. You're not going to like it."

"Really? I'm surprised. Because so far this conversation has been a barrel of laughs."

He ignores me. "Like I told you, Simmons is confessing to conspiracy to commit a number of murders."

"So?"

"So Rachel Morehouse isn't one of them; he says he has no idea who killed her. There's no reason he would lie about that; we have him dead to rights twelve times over. And what he said had the ring of truth; he even claimed that Jim Wolford didn't know what was going on, that Simmons dealt with Stal exclusively."

"You got any other terrible things to tell me? Maybe you did a biopsy on me without my realizing it, and the results are in?"

He smiles. "No, I'm done. And I am sorry about this, but it's for a greater cause."

"Yeah. That makes me feel much better, and I'm sure Tony Wasserman will be just thrilled as he spends the rest of his life in prison."

With no Unser or other federal official to testify, all I can do to wrap up my case is call Pete Stanton to the stand.

Pete can talk about both the other night's events on the plane and the attempted drive-by shooting that resulted in Marrero's death. He can't describe the conspiracy behind the people being flown in. Even if he knew the reason for it, he wouldn't be able to talk about it because, well . . . the president of the United States.

The two incidents in combination convey the point that people were trying to kill me. I can imply that it was to stop my investigation, but by now I have been so irritating that the jurors probably want to kill me as well.

I keep Pete on the stand for almost an hour, mostly so I can delay saying the words that I finally have to say when I let him off.

"Your Honor, the defense rests."

This has not been a complicated case," Strickland says, starting her closing argument.

"Yes, I know, Mr. Carpenter has done his best to make it complicated, and I must tell you I was as fascinated by his efforts as you must have been. But it was all smoke and mirrors, and it didn't change any of the basic facts.

"The evidence shows very clearly that Mr. Wasserman had the means and the motive to kill Rachel Morehouse. He was living in her house; he had come there in an attempt to get in her good graces, so that he could receive a substantial part of the fortune she was leaving behind.

"When he found out that was not to be, he couldn't deal with it. Using his knowledge of chemistry and of her failing health, he prepared a particularly lethal dose of poison, one that he knew would kill her.

"But he wasn't careful enough, possibly because of his anger. He left traces of the chemical behind, in his car and his room, and that proves his guilt as surely as if he was on camera committing the crime.

"You heard the evidence from the capable forensics people who analyzed it. You heard from Rachel Morehouse's close friend Susan Wolford that things were not going well between Rachel and Mr. Wasserman. Rachel told her that; she wanted it to work, but it just didn't. What Rachel didn't know was that it would result in her death.

"But Mr. Carpenter didn't focus on any of that. Instead he regaled us with tales of a criminal conspiracy within Wasserman Equities. To be honest, I don't know how much of that is true. I haven't been spending time finding out; I've been too busy here, trying to convict the murderer of Rachel Morehouse.

"But for the moment, let's give Mr. Carpenter the benefit of the doubt and say it's all true, every word of it. Let's say there was a criminal conspiracy in that company, involving drugs and planes and rest stops on Route Seventeen and drive-by shootings and whatever.

"And let's go a step further. Let's say that the people behind the conspiracy were afraid that Mr. Carpenter would expose their evil deeds and foil their plots. And they tried, and fortunately failed, to silence him.

"So what? What does that have to do with Rachel Morehouse and the stepson that she refused to leave her fortune to? Can't both things exist simultaneously? Does the fact that a company was committing criminal acts mean that Anthony Wasserman couldn't have murdered Rachel Morehouse?

"Does that make any sense at all?

"If the crimes that Mr. Carpenter is alleging at Wasserman Equities are real, then I hope that someday soon another jury, sitting where you are sitting, holds the criminals responsible.

"That will be their job, but that is not your job. You are here to make a judgment as to the guilt or innocence of Anthony Wasserman, and I would submit that we have provided you all the facts, not theories and suppositions, but facts, to help you make that decision.

"Thank you."

Getting up to start my closing argument isn't the worst feeling I have during a case.

Just to be clear, it's a terrible, awful, miserable feeling. I know that this is the last chance I will have to make our case, and that if I can't do it effectively now, I'll never be able to.

But as bad as it is, finishing the closing argument is even worse. Because then it is truly out of my hands, nothing I can say or think of or come up with will matter, because the jury won't hear any of it.

"Ladies and gentleman, you're in the home stretch. You've heard a lot of talking, and there isn't much more to come. I will speak for a while, I'll try to be as brief as I can, and then Judge Lofton will instruct you on the task you have ahead.

"For the moment, let's talk about what Judge Lofton will say. I have been through a great many of these trials, and I've heard a lot of charges given by a lot of judges. I think that I can say with certainty that included in the one you will hear is an instruction concerning reasonable doubt.

"You don't have to decide guilt or innocence; that's not your job. You have to decide whether guilt has been proven beyond a reasonable doubt. That's a high bar, and I would submit that the prosecution hasn't come close to clearing it.

"We have presented to you absolutely incontrovertible evidence of a massive and violent criminal conspiracy at Wasserman Equities. It wasn't me opining on it, spinning wild tales in the hope that you'll believe it.

"You've heard it from homicide captains, and state cops, and DEA agents. These are not people who generally testify for the defense, but here they were, telling you the truth. Telling you the facts.

"You've heard testimony that Rachel Morehouse was obsessed with learning what was going on at Wasserman Equities, the company she inherited. She was ill with cancer and heart disease, yet there she was, digging into the corruption that she found.

"Do you think she had a sudden desire to learn about business? Was she planning to go back to school for her MBA? Of course not. She was going to make sure the media reported what she learned because she wanted to break up the conspiracy forever.

"She was a hero, and they killed her for it.

"So with all the facts you have heard about drug dealing, and smuggling, and murder, is it not reasonable to consider the possibility that the woman who was trying to uncover it was a victim of it as well?

"Can you possibly say that the criminals who showed no hesitation to kill didn't add Rachel Morehouse to their list when she was a mortal threat to them? Of course not.

"Instead of pointing the finger where it should be pointed, Ms. Strickland points it at Mr. Wasserman. And who is he? A man who has devoted his life to teaching, who has never demonstrated any interest in wealth, who has never committed a violent act, who has never been charged with a crime or arrested, who simply responded when his stepmother expressed an interest in strengthening their family relationship.

"This is the prosecution's version of a cold-blooded killer. They've sifted through all the actual killers, and drug dealers, and this is who they've targeted.

"You have a chance to fix this. Not entirely, and that is unfortunate. You cannot give back the time that Anthony Wasserman has spent in jail waiting for this trial to happen and to conclude. You cannot undo the stress he has suffered as the State of New Jersey tried to deprive him of his freedom.

"But you can give him justice. You can send the message that law-abiding people cannot be treated like this, that other law-abiding people like yourselves will not allow it.

"I urge you to make sure that justice is served. Thank you."

I look at Tony Wasserman as I get back to the defense table. I would like to say something to ease his anxiety, but I can't, because I'm too anxious myself.

And nothing I say will matter because, from this moment on, no one gives a damn what Andy Carpenter says or thinks.

That's the way the system works.

Ordinarily, waiting for a verdict is excruciating on two levels. One is the obvious . . . the tension is incredible, the anxiety level off the charts.

The other horror is, strangely, the opposite. It is boring; nothing happens until it happens, and sometimes days go by with no news of any kind.

Today is not one of those boring days, and I receive the news courtesy of Pete Stanton: "Carl Simmons was killed in his home last night. One bullet through the head."

"How the hell could they let that happen?"

"He was under house arrest, Andy. The goal is to keep him inside, not to stop someone else from getting in."

Once again, as happened when Jim Wolford committed suicide, I am not heartbroken by the loss to society. And it has no effect on our case; the jury is sequestered and won't even know about it.

So life goes on . . . unless your name is Carl Simmons.

I can only assume that the man they call Stal has cleaned up the loose ends. It could have been disastrous for Stal had Simmons told his story under oath. Stal wouldn't even have any way of knowing that the authorities are on to his operation; he could think that killing Simmons keeps it in place.

When I tell Laurie what has happened, along with my view of it, she says, "Stal could see you as one of those loose ends too."

"I love that upbeat attitude," I say, while knowing she's right.

Like always, I'm not sure whether I want the jury to come back quickly, or to take a long time. I guess if I were pushed, I'd say I hope for a lengthy deliberation. Our case was the complicated one, so I'd want the jury to study it carefully. If they reach a verdict right away, it might mean that they've rejected our version of the case out of hand.

I generally like to be alone while waiting, but for some reason this time I'm feeling a bit different. Maybe it's because I'm usually pessimistic about the verdict, and this time I have some optimism. I don't want to have optimism, though, because pessimism has worked well for me in the past. So I need to get myself some pessimism.

What I actually need is therapy.

But I agree to Laurie's suggestion that we go out to dinner, once the jury has stopped deliberating for the day. Ricky is sleeping over at a friend's house, so Laurie and I go out. Nothing fancy, just a local diner.

Since we never do something like this during a verdict watch, we're sort of breaking new ground. I don't want to discuss the case, but it's all either of us is thinking about. It's the elephant in the diner, so I don't resist when Laurie asks the key question:

"So who killed Rachel Morehouse?"

"I honestly don't know. Maybe Marrero, or Callison, or Stal. But that house was not one you could just walk up to, not during the day. That's why I've always thought it must have been someone that Rachel knew, someone who had access, and . . ." I stop talking.

"What is it?"

"I know who killed her. Let's get the check."

The lights are on in Susan Wolford's house when we arrive. We ring the bell, but there is no answer. Music is playing from somewhere in the house, so we ring the bell a few more times and bang on the door to try to get a response.

None is forthcoming.

I try the door handle and it is unlocked. "Should we go in?"

"We don't have probable cause," Laurie says.

"We're not cops looking to make an arrest or execute a search warrant. What could happen?"

She nods. "Okay."

I'm actually a little nervous about going in because of what we might find. "You bring a gun with you?" I ask, but I then see that Laurie is already holding one in her hand. "I guess you did."

I open the door and we go in, cautiously. Laurie leads the way because she's Laurie, and I'm me. We walk about ten feet in, and Laurie says, in a strange tone, "Oh, Andy."

I look and see what the "Oh, Andy" was about; Susan Wolford lies in a pool of blood at the entrance to her den. She's facedown with the bullet hole in the back of her head; she was running from her killer.

Laurie, in the ready position with her gun, scans the rooms to see if the killer might still be present. Suddenly we hear a crashing noise coming from the front of the house. We head to-ward the sound, with Laurie leading the way, again for obvious reasons.

We go through the open door and look to the left, toward the noise. Marcus Clark is holding a person who must outweigh him by thirty pounds. Marcus is throwing that person against the wall of the house, and the person's head is arriving at the wall first. Hence the thumping noise.

After two more tosses, Marcus grabs the guy to throw him again.

"Marcus, that's enough." He looks toward Laurie, and she says, "Okay, one more."

Marcus obliges. The guy then slumps to the ground, clearly out cold.

I go over to him and look down. "Stal . . . never mess with Andy Carpenter."

get the call at 3:00 P.M. on the third day of deliberations. The jury has a verdict.

The length of time they took means conclusively that we either won or lost; we won't know which until the verdict is read.

Laurie comes with me to the courthouse and takes a seat in the gallery. Eddie Dowd is waiting for me at the defense table, looking stricken with anxiety. He's a former football Giants player who played in an NFC title game, and he says the pressure in that game doesn't compare to the pressure of waiting for a verdict.

Tony is brought in and asks what we think. I say what I always say, "I think we'll know in a few minutes."

Eddie nods in solemn agreement.

Judge Lofton comes in and asks for the jury, who quickly file in. I'm sure everything is happening quickly, but it seems like slow motion to me.

The judge asks Tony to stand, and Eddie and I do as well, flanking him on either side. My legs are made of rubber, and not particularly sturdy rubber.

The verdict sheet is brought to the judge, who silently reads it and then hands it to the court clerk to read aloud. The clerk clears her throat, which seems to take about an hour and a half.

"We the jury, in the case of *New Jersey versus Anthony Wasserman,* as to count one, the homicide of Mrs. Rachel Morehouse, find the defendant, Anthony Wasserman, not guilty of the crime of first-degree homicide."

Tony slumps to the table; it's hard to imagine the stress he must have been feeling. Eddie puts his hand on Tony's shoulder, then Tony stands and hugs Eddie, then me.

"I will never be able to thank you enough," Tony says.

The gallery is in something of an uproar, so Judge Lofton calls for quiet, thanks the jury, then dismisses them.

When it's all over, Kathryn Strickland comes over to shake my hand and says, a smile on her face, "Your reputation definitely preceded you."

We almost always have our post-trial victory party at Charlie's. They give us the private room upstairs, the food is great, and they let dogs in for the occasion.

Representing the human race tonight are Laurie, Tony, Eddie, Sam, Corey, Willie Miller and Sondra, his wife, the Bubeleh Brigade, Pete Stanton, and Vince Sanders. Pete and Vince obviously were not part of the defense team, but the food and beer are free, so they're here.

The canine contingent includes Tara, Hunter, Lion, and Simon Garfunkel. Sebastian chose to sleep this one out.

We put this party together in a hurry; we only got the verdict yesterday. Tony is anxious to take Lion and get home; classes at his school have already started, and he wants to get back to his teaching.

I haven't had time to talk to him since the verdict, and his questions center on how I knew that Susan Wolford killed Rachel.

"I wasn't positive," I say, "but there was a lot that pointed to it. For one thing, she kept lying. She said you were home when she visited Rachel that morning, but you told me you weren't. She said that Rachel told her things were going badly with you, but that wasn't true either. She also said that Rachel was happy with the state of the business.

"When people lie, there's always a reason."

"Is that all?"

"No. Susan Wolford had been a nurse, so she would have easily been able to effectively administer the injection. And I think she was having an affair with Simmons; Rachel had said that Simmons was too interested in married women.

"When I went to see Simmons in his office, right after I left Sam said he called Wolford at home. But I had just seen Wolford getting off the elevator at the office, so Simmons must have been calling Susan.

"I think Simmons was at Rachel's house with Susan that day, and he was the one that the neighbor heard arguing with Rachel. I think Susan stayed behind and killed her because she was afraid Rachel was going to blow up the business and destroy her lifestyle.

"I also think that Susan killed her husband; he didn't commit suicide. Why would he? Even Simmons said he had nothing to do with the criminality. Susan was afraid of what he might say that could ruin everything, so she killed him and made it look like a suicide. And that way she and Simmons could have been together."

"What happened to Stal?" Tony asks.

"Last I saw him, his head was bouncing off the front of a house. But I'm told he's going to pull through; I imagine that once his head clears, the FBI's questioning of him will be rather intense."

Tony just shakes his head in amazement. "This has been quite a summer vacation for me."

"So you had fun?"

"A blast. But Lion and I won't be back for a while."

"I'm on the board of the charitable foundation that Rachel set up. I get to pick another board member, and it's going to be you. That kind of money can do great things, and you can do it from Indiana."

He nods. "I would like that."

Lion is in the middle of the room, wrestling with Tara and Simon Garfunkel. "I almost hate to take him away from his friends," Tony says.

"Maybe you should get him a friend of his own."

"I think I'll do that." Tony shakes my hand. "Everybody needs a friend."